Hattie's Homestead

The Other Legend

Book One

Hattie's Homestead

The Other Legend

Book One

By Marion Grace

Marion Grace
Leafgate Publishing LLC
9249 S. Broadway #200-831
Highlands Ranch CO 80129
Copyright © 2018 by Marion Grace
All rights reserved.
ISBN 978-1-7327760-0-5

Front Cover photo of Tucumcari Mountain: I, the copyright holder of this work, release this work into the public domain. This applies worldwide. In some countries this may not be legally possible; if so: *I grant anyone the right to use this work for any purpose, without any conditions, unless such conditions are required by law.*https://commons.wikimedia.org /wiki/ File:TucMt.jpg

Front cover portraits used by permission from B. Andres family.
Front cover image of building taken by author.

Back Cover photo of rail road tracks. This image was taken by the author.

Printed in the United States of America

Leafgate Publishing '

Dedication

"This book is dedicated to the countless unfulfilled lives and devastated souls who came before me, and the LGBTQ people who endure suffering today.

I am extremely grateful for my loving partner (now wife), loving siblings, and the acceptance of many straight people in our community.

Hattie's Homestead
The Other Legend

Book One

Table of Contents

Chapter One – Amarillo Summer 1904 1

Chapter Two – City Hall..23

Chapter Three – Betting the Homestead......................37

Chapter Four – Finding Help 42

Chapter Five – Picking Stones from Your Heart.........59

Chapter Six – Where's Earl?.......................................81

Chapter Seven – The Rabbit and the Cane 99

Chapter Eight – The Ghost 121

Chapter Nine – I Can Do This 137

Chapter Ten – Ladies and Gentlemen........................161

Eleven – Legend of Tucumcari Mountain 173

Chapter Twelve – Empty Handed...............................183

Chapter Thirteen – Pale Blue Ribbon 193

Chapter Fourteen – No, Not Fine...............................211

Chapter Fifteen – Willy Quinn's Place......................231

Chapter Sixteen – Like a Carousel.............................241

Chapter Seventeen – The Poem 251

Chapter Eighteen – Credible Reasons........................267

Nineteen – A Pair of Hankies 285

Chapter One – Amarillo
Summer 1904

Hattie Moore stared aimlessly down the cottonwood and oak-lined drive that stretched a good quarter-mile from her parent's front porch to where it then gently sloped down to meet the parched dirt road that leads five miles into Amarillo. With her legs stretched out beside her, she occupied the full width of her parent's porch swing. Her left elbow slopped over the armrest with her head propped up on her hand making her face bunch up on one side. Her mother wouldn't approve, of course, it made her appear lazy, bored, and most of all unladylike. She didn't care, but listened for her mother's, or their maid, Cassie's, approaching footsteps anyway.

She had just finished reading the novel "The Virginian: A Horseman of the Plains," a story about a man from Virginia who became a foreman at the Sunk Creek Ranch in Wyoming and in the process learned the ways of the west; to be self-reliant, courageous, rugged, and independent.

Hattie switched over and slouched on her right side. She felt both bored and irritable. It wouldn't be long before she would be shuffled off again to that Dallas finishing school for girls, and already detested every future mind-numbing minute of it. It was 1904, she just turned eighteen and was chewing on the fact that at least this would be the last year she would be compelled to attend.

There were many times when she wished that her parents could not afford for her to grow up to be a lady; just the idea of it made her feel pinched both physically and emotionally. Those cinched-up dresses only made her feel less capable of performing any worthwhile activities. And, those insipid rules of behavior, imposed by her mother and southern society, were at best silly and altogether utterly insane. She did not want to be protected under a parasol from the sun or versed in useless English poetry. Her peers at school could only manage to blither on about Paris fashions, catching a beau, idly gossiping about one another or sharing dirt about the school staff. For Hattie, finishing school was about as stimulating as cold grits.

She never fit in at the Wainwright Finishing School for Girls nor did she aspire to. Each day was equally tedious for both Hattie and her frustrated school attendants charged with turning Hattie into one of their respected alumni. She rarely held herself quite right, correctly daubed her napkin at the edges of her mouth, or handled items with a delicate hand. When the other girls swooned and giggled over pictures of this or that, Hattie just rolled her eyes.

Hattie was not stupid and could out perform any of her classmates in any form of etiquette and in every social protocol. She could, if she wanted to, glide into a ballroom attracting the attention of all the assembled gentlemen with her natural born beauty and effortless grace. She also could turn the heads of all the jealous debutantes. And, just to prove a point, that is exactly what she did at the last Christmas ball.

When she entered the room, every eye was on her. People who were chatting stopped midsentence, turning to see where everyone

else was looking. At first, the girls could not understand who let in an uninvited female guest; especially one that made them seem as bland and enticing as boiled lettuce. It was only after several moments passed, when Mrs. Wainwright said, "Good evening Miss Moore," that the gaggle of pouty-faced classmates knew – this was no outsider; it was Hattie!

If one didn't know that the floor was flat one would swear it was slanted towards Hattie and all the men had lost their footing. Throughout the evening, she introduced herself by her given name "Harriet" instead of "Hattie," and all the rich and handsome young men openly competed for a place on her dance card. Many of them acted like well-dressed baboons vying to refill her punch glass each time she took a sip.

Within an hour she had made her point; she outdid them all with barely a thought. It was a game she could play and easily win if she wanted to, but she did not.

There was nothing more she could learn from this institution, and finally everyone knew it. From then on Hattie only participated in enough school activities so to not embarrass her mother. When school recessed for the summer, everyone was relieved.

At home Hattie immediately reverted to being rough around the edges and planned to stay that way as long she could get away with it. Her mother worried like a hen but scolding never worked. When she warned Hattie that she would never find a suitable husband, she would not raise a single eyebrow. Her mother felt

that becoming a lady was really a practical endeavor. It was well and good to marry for love, but why not attract prospects from the best young men in Texas or parts East? With Hattie's natural beauty she only needed to half try to find both love and a financially secure future. Why was this so difficult to understand?

In fact, Hattie did understand and, at some level, appreciated her mother's concern for her future. After all, her mother had lost her parents, two brothers, a sister-in-law, and four nephews, in the great hurricane while vacationing in Galveston and its three-year anniversary was coming this September. Hattie recalled that as soon as her mother could, she travelled there to claim the family remains. But learned that because there were thousands of deaths, officials resorted to building funeral pyres on the beaches to dispose of the bodies. The experience changed her mother forever.

Hattie's father hoped that the focus on Hattie's future would be a way for her mother to "concentrate on the living." However, she refused to believe that her mother's notion of her future life was the only life to which she could aspire.

Her interests had always taken another path. Ever since she was a small girl she drew near to anyone telling stories of how it was in the old days. Just about everyone over the age of forty had something to say about "The Old West." Their tales of the frontier made most girls her age shudder, but they only peaked Hattie's imagination.

Most of the older men's stories focused on feats of bravery and skill against the elements, the Natives, or the Mexicans. They boasted and proudly shared their history, with any willing listener,

even a girl. They even lent her copies of their old dime novels of the West as if those stories validated their own.

The older women also talked about those same years, but in quiet voices. Their stories often recalled the endless toil, the sicknesses that stole their children's lives, the dirt, and the loneliness caused by the great empty distances between neighbors. Their pain was not expressed by their spoken words, but with their solemn delivery and the sadness in their eyes expressing that part of their souls left hollow.

When these women told their stories, Hattie truly felt sympathetic for their plights, but their stories seemed irrelevant to her. If given a chance, these would not be her story. Living the adventure had to outbalance the sacrifices, didn't it? Hattie rationalized that possibly these women were once like the girls at Wainwright. They just couldn't cope with the challenges of relying on their own wits or their own hard labor. They must have started out soft; girls who never considered climbing a tree, throwing rocks, or watching a horse being shoed.

As Hattie grew older, her opinions became more steadfast; somehow it had to be different for her. Given the opportunity, she would gladly be a pioneer woman struggling with frontier life and its harsh uncertain terms than struggling into a damn corset. She mused that if she had the means to do it, she would hitch up that wagon in the barn and head out West tomorrow. She'd tame some piece of frontier land and nail up a sign, "Hattie's Homestead," yes sir, "Hattie's Homestead."

Hattie's eyes watched a stray grasshopper jumping across the porch while she pondered the question of how much untamed west remained out there. She speculated that this subject was purposely omitted from the Wainwright syllabus.

Hattie turned her attention to the sounds of her father finishing up in the front parlor. Today she would accompany him to meet the train in Amarillo and was glad to be away from her mother's nervous glances.

About halfway into town her father handed the reins to Hattie, which he had done since she was about ten years old. Initially, her mother did not approve, but her father insisted that any child of his would know how to handle horses. And, he reminded his wife that long ago she could drive a team as well as any of his men. Eventually they reached a compromise that Hattie could drive the buggy and wagons as long as there were only two horses in the team. More importantly, Mr. Moore would take the reins back before they got into town. A proper lady would never drive when a perfectly able man was present.

Once Hattie took the reins, Mr. Moore began explaining to her the many details of the unusually large shipment of pipe his irrigation company would be receiving from Ohio. She was used to this and long ago concluded that this was how he organized his thoughts. The details were seldom interesting, but she enjoyed these short trips with him. He seemed happier when she listened to him talk about the business. Besides, he never tried to change her the way her mother did.

A light rain passed through two days ago and now the sunbaked mud crunched under the wheels of their wagon. Hattie's father carefully maneuvered his rig between several wagons near the bustling depot.

Her father pulled a letter out from his inside pocket and glanced at it to ensure he understood the delivery particulars. But he already knew them by heart. Mr. Lyles, at the Henry Pipe Company, wrote that the firm would send Earl Babcock, a young handling manager's assistant, to help with Mr. Moore's shipment. Initially, Mr. Moore felt a little irritated. He knew his own men were quite capable of dealing with the load. As he saw it, it was a waste even though he wasn't being billed for it.

Hattie and her father walked towards the loading area. As they got closer Mr. Moore could see that his company's wagons were empty, and the crew was just idly sitting by a pipe-filled railroad car. Two of them were busy talking to a young woman, one was rolling a cigarette, and the fourth decided to take a nap in the back of one of the wagons. His pace quickened, and Hattie had to hurry to catch up.

"So, where's this Earl Babcock who was sent to meet us?" he bellowed at the men. They all quickly straightened up. "We don't know sir. We've been here over an hour and no one's showed up yet."

"And did anyone think to ask around for him?" The men just silently looked down at their boots. "Honestly, I've seen dead lizards with more gumption than the lot of you."

Mr. Moore hated to wait for anything or anyone, especially a northerner, so he began asking around for Earl. "Do you know if a young guy named Earl is around?" he asked a porter. Then he asked the switchman the same thing. "Well, I thought I saw him go into the office a few minutes ago. You might catch him there."

"Thanks," he returned.

With Hattie close behind, Mr. Moore walked in the office and found two men behind the counter. One was a portly elderly man shuffling through papers, obviously looking for something in particular. Behind him was a young man obviously looking for something in a cabinet. The younger man, not knowing others were present in the room, barked at the older man.

"Damn it! I'm bleeding like a goddamn stuck pig over here. Get your fat ass over here to help me find the bandages! If you don't help me I'm gonna stick those papers up where you haven't been able to wipe for the last thirty years."

Mr. Moore was not amused and a bit embarrassed over the colorful words his daughter just heard. He abruptly butted in. "Listen Earl, you are Earl I assume? I'm Tyler Moore. You better get yourself fixed and ready for work at car 289 in five minutes or you'll never see your beloved North again!" He then turned to his daughter and said, "Hattie, come." He motioned her through the door and slammed it shut behind him.

The young man, holding his cut thumb, stood shocked as his eyes followed them past the windows facing the platform. "Who the hell was that, Tom?" he asked.

"Apparently, he's Tyler Aaaa Moore," Tom mocked then asked, "what business you got with him?"

Earl replied. "Beats me, and I've never been up north. Say, where are those bandages? I better get out there in case the boss signed me up to do something he forgot to tell me about. You know Mr. Gary; it's never his fault when something gets balled up."

Earl quickly wrapped his thumb and trotted down to car 289. Mr. Moore, standing next to the stacked flatbed, immediately bellowed, "Earl, what are you standin' there for? Your boss said you were in charge of unloading my order."

Up until now Earl's only experience with unloading freight was when he accompanied several cars of cattle being shipped to Amarillo. All he had to do was whoop and holler the boxed herd down the wooden chutes and help verify that the buyer's counters came up with the same numbers his ranch boss wrote on the invoice. This load of pipe might take more figuring.

Earl climbed up the metal rungs of the train car and surveyed the load. He concluded they could simply unfasten the hold-down straps and get a couple of men on top to hand down the thirty-foot pieces over the top, one at a time. He positioned himself with the other men and started to unload.

After about ten minutes, Mr. Moore became very irritated. "You fool. At this rate it will take us four days and this here train is

going to start moving again in four hours. You better think of something fast or your boss will have one less employee!"

Earl quickly surveyed the yard and noticed a neatly stacked shipment of lumber that looked like two-by-six-by-twelve's. He told one man to position one of their wagons parallel to the car and remove its side rails. He then got the other two men to bring over some planks. Earl then laid a bridge of planks from the higher train car to the lower wagon. Next, he removed the two center flatbed stakes leaving one stake on each side, holding the load. Mr. Moore figured out what Earl was about to attempt and turned to Hattie, "Well this is more like it. I bet his boss pays him by the hour and Earl wanted to see if he could stretch out his time and get away with it."

Earl told one of the men to get into position at one end of the load of pipe as he positioned himself at the other. "Look," he paused and then asked, "What's your name?"

"Leroy, he replied."

"Look, Leroy, all this pipe isn't gonna fit in this one wagon. When I say stop we gotta put the stakes back in these sleeves here. Understand?" The man nodded his head. "Now when I say pull, you pull up your stake, OK?" Again, the man nodded.

"All right then. One, two, three, pull." The stakes were pulled up and the irrigation pipe began flowing down the wooden bridge like dozens of pencils rolling off an uneven table. When the wagon was about full he yelled at Leroy to push the stakes back into position. The first wagon was hauled away, and the second wagon

took its place. Earl felt very good about his accomplishment and smiled at Leroy who was equally pleased.

"Okay. Ready to go again. One, two, three, pull." Just then a man came running towards them. "Stop. Stop!" he screamed. Mr. Moore turned and saw a desperate young man in a suit holding his hat on his head with one hand and waving what looked like a dinner napkin in the other. He was now right in front of the team and continued to frantically shout and wave his napkin.

The frightened horses bucked at the sight of the madman causing the planks beneath the pipes to angle and fall. Leroy reached down to save the falling bridge but lost his balance and fell off the car. He barely saved himself from being crushed by jumping under the flatbed as the remaining pipes avalanched to the ground below. The crashing metal sounded like hundreds of bells being thrown over a cliff. It could be heard a half mile away causing the whole community to see what happened.

The crowd stood in silence as the last pipe dangled precariously off the flatbed and then it too dropped with a single clank. For a few seconds, Mr. Moore, his men, Earl, Hattie, and the suited man stood in silent disbelief. Mr. Moore's face flushed with boiling anger as he turned to the stranger, "Who the hell are you? Just who in the hell are you?" he screamed and spat out at the man.

The terrified man, still panting from the run, stuttered "Earl, Earl Bab-Babcock s-sir. Mr. Lyles sent me with the load. He, he said he sent word." Mr. Moore then turned to Earl, still on top of the train car. "And you?" he said, much more softly. "Earl, Earl Curtis, sir. I work here with the train company; my third week."

11

From under the flatbed, Leroy exploded into laughter. The other men tried to shut him up by scowling at him, but it only made it worse. "Leroy, Leroy shut up," the men coaxed. Leroy looked at Earl and concentrated on keeping a straight face.

Earl saw Leroy's eyes bugging out and knew he was about to explode again. Caught up with the humor of the situation, Earl exploded into laughter and was bent over laughing as hordes of townsfolk gathered to view the spectacle.

A large man with grease up to both elbows pushed his way to the front. He wore gray-bibbed coveralls and an engineer's cap pulled low across his brow. Most people recognized Mr. Gary and immediately pulled back to let him through. When he got to the front the crowd went silent, even Leroy and the two Earls stood in silence.

Mr. Gary faced the crowd and surveyed the first three rows of gawkers. "Okay. Jim, Carter, Millard, Chauncey, Frank, Whitey, Hank, Todd, and Gilley – you all stay. The rest of you go on about your business. We got work to do here. Now Earl, you...." The suited man with the napkin stepped forward. "No, not you. Earl, you move both teams ahead about twenty feet. Men, make a fire-bucket line from this mess over to the wagons. Let's go."

The wagons were loaded in about twenty minutes and the big excitement for the week was over. Mr. Moore instructed his men to go on with the loads and he would follow later. Next, he turned his attention to the Earl in the city suit who was now nervously tying and untying knots in the napkin. He pulled him by the arm some distance from his daughter, while Mr. Gary went about his business talking with the engineer and the head yardman. This left only Hattie and Earl Curtis standing on the loading platform.

Earl watched Mr. Moore scold and wag his finger at the other Earl but couldn't hear what he was saying. Hattie sat down on a bench under the eaves and looked towards Earl Curtis. He needed a haircut. The front fell over his brow while the back of his hair was bluntly cut above the collar. Hattie quickly assumed that either a friend cut his hair, or he did his own.

As he stood watching the men, he unconsciously combed it back with his fingers. His face looked like he was in his early twenties, but his body was that of a fully filled-out man. Hattie also observed that his suspenders formed a "Y" between his muscular shoulder blades.

He turned to Hattie. "Well, today was quite a day. I hope your father simmers down so at least your evening won't be so bad." He looked at her face, her hair, her eyes, and then her mouth. Suddenly he felt self-conscious and looked down at his feet.

Hattie replied, "Oh, he'll be all right. I think he enjoys getting stirred up every now and then." Then she looked down at Earl's bandaged thumb. "Oh look" as she gently grabbed his hand. "This bandage is useless. Come on, let me fix it for you while my father is occupied."

They went back into the office where Hattie tended to Earl's wound. As Hattie finished the bandage, Hattie's father stepped into the room. Earl saw Mr. Moore walk in and fully expected to be scolded, but it didn't happen.

Instead, Mr. Moore walked over to Earl, rolled a cigarette, then lit it. He tipped the brim of his hat up a bit and said, "Earl, I guess you tried your best. You know, the first load went great. You've got a head on your shoulders. And don't worry, I caught Mr. Gary outside and this won't go against ya." He then turned to Hattie. "Well, we best be getting on now." Hattie started towards the door, but then Mr. Moore stopped and extended his hand to Earl. Earl smiled, took Mr. Moore's hand, and gave it a good pump.

After the Moores left the office, Earl opened his right hand and found a five-dollar note Mr. Moore passed to him during the handshake. He slowly unfolded it and it felt good having that extra money in his hand, but his heart felt even better.

On his next day off, Earl spent four of his five extra dollars on a couple of new shirts, one for work and one for whatever. He also splurged on a real barbershop haircut. He didn't know if he would see Hattie again, but just in case, he wanted to look more presentable than he had at their first meeting.

As it turned out, he saw Hattie many times over the summer because she found every excuse in the world to go into Amarillo with her father, especially when he had business at the depot.

She relished hearing Earl's stories of working on the big northwest Texas ranches. When he told her he was proud to be seen with the prettiest girl around she felt her face turn red. She quickly changed the subject and asked how he ended up working for the railroad.

He playfully kicked up a patch of dirt with his boot and then told her he got his railroad experience working in the roundhouses at the Abilene and Lubbock railyards. That's where he learned to take apart and service locomotive-brake assemblies, car couplers, and journal boxes.

But he utterly captivated her when he said enthusiastically that railroads were growing at a tremendous rate throughout the New Mexico Territory and he could easily pick up work out there. But he also wanted to try homesteading, he wanted to be a pioneer!

With each meeting, each unhurried walk around town, each conversation about the past and speculating about the future, they became closer. Earl seemed very interested in how Mr. Moore built up his business and told Hattie he had the ambition, the willingness, and even the stubbornness, to succeed.

It was the second week in August when Hattie's mother cheerfully announced at the supper table, "Hattie, the two new dresses I ordered for you arrived from New York today. I don't want Mrs. Kemp, or any of those uppity Dallas women thinking that your father's business isn't doing well." Hattie did not respond – she was in shock.

She had totally buried any thoughts of finishing school for the entire summer. She had successfully deluded herself into believing that school was no longer a mandate.

Her mother continued to babble, "The coat hasn't arrived yet, but you could make do with your blue one for a little while. I'll

send the new one as soon as it arrives." Her mother finally noticed that Hattie did not share her enthusiasm. "Hattie, dear, I'm so sorry the coat didn't arrive at the same time as the dresses, really I am." Hattie didn't look at her parents and politely excused herself from the table. As he watched his daughter escape up the stairs, her father sensed there was more going on than issues with the new wardrobe.

Hattie's mother began to get up, but Tyler motioned for her to stay. "She's at an age where she has to do some thinking on her own. You know that. Besides, maybe she's gone a little sweet on that Earl feller."

She rolled her eyes and sighed, "Well I can't say that I'm unhappy that she finally turned her head towards a beau, even if he's nothing like the sort I would choose for her. At least she's started looking and soon she'll be in the company of better prospects."

He wanted to change the mood in the room. "Did I smell Cassie's peach pie earlier, or was my imagination goin' wild?"

Over the next few weeks, Hattie tried to contact Earl. She finally found out from Leroy that he had been sent sixty miles south to Newton to work on an engine whose brakes had failed. Leroy also said that the locomotive caused considerable damage to a couple of freight cars that were unfortunately in the way when the brakes failed. Earl would try to salvage any of the more

expensive components and to bring them back. The rest would be scrapped locally.

Three more days would pass before she would find an employee who would get a message to Earl. The worker told Hattie that he was scheduled to go to Newton the next day, but due to last minute changes, he didn't leave until several days later.

Once in Newton, the brakeman reached deep into a seven-foot pile of twisted rubble to hand the letter to Earl. "Thanks," Earl replied, but in the dim lighting and cramped quarters, he barely made out who wrote the letter. After a few moments he emerged into the light and told a waiting Mexican laborer, "nothing worth saving in there. Go ahead and move the whole mess to the scrap pile."

Earl walked to the nearby workshed and sat down on an upended ten-gallon oil can. He reached into his back pocket and took out a large red handkerchief to wipe the grease and ash off his hands and face before opening the letter:

> *Dear Earl,*
>
> *I am so sorry I could not say goodbye to you in person. I leave on Tuesday to return to the Wainwright Finishing School for Girls in Dallas and didn't know when you would be back. My parents ardently wish for me to return to school, but it is not mine.*
>
> *I hope you do not think me too bold to say I truly enjoyed your company and I miss you now. Our*

meeting was meant to be, and I am distressed to be forced apart from you.

Someday, I hope that we can continue our relationship, but for now I can only tell you that you are in my fondest thoughts. I wish you God Speed.

Hattie Moore

Earl slowly folded the letter placing it in his shirt pocket. He stood, took a few steps outside, and leaned his tired body against the door frame. He watched the silhouette of a jack rabbit running down the tracks and said to himself, "Now what am I gonna do?"

Chapter Two – City Hall

When Hattie arrived in Dallas, she was depressed, angry, and didn't care who noticed. There wasn't a single thing she wanted or needed in this town, this county, or this institute of fallacious learning. She stewed for hours wondering why her parents were so set on making her into someone she was not unless it was for their own selfish reasons. If she married the right man it would elevate her mother's status and that infuriated her. She was not an object and was not about to be prepped and groomed like prize livestock for auction.

For the next two months she was either stewing over her compulsory lessons of refinement or was brooding because Earl was so far away. Why hadn't she heard from him? Was she too bold? Was she too much of one thing, not enough of another? But, what?

The staff couldn't do anything to motivate her to keep up with her lessons or show at least a feigned interest with the social activities. Even Mrs. Martin's private lesson on "Culture Begins with the Cultured Woman" had any effect. Hattie knew this would eventually get back to her parents, but they were at fault, and she didn't care.

On the second Sunday in October a messenger delivered a sealed envelope to the school addressed to Miss H. Moore. One of the first-year students was instructed to bring it directly to Hattie's room.

There were several other girls in her room who had gathered to talk with Hattie's roommate, so she left in search of privacy. The main study was empty, so she slipped in and found a chair concealed from view. She opened the letter and her heart raced with excitement.

My Dear Hattie,

I am here in Dallas but must leave very soon. I must speak with you. Meet me at the City Hall tomorrow at noon. I will wait for you.

Earl

She wanted to scream and race up and down the stairs with joy. But logic forced her to remain calm and think of a way to disappear for a few hours tomorrow.

She could easily get to City Hall by walking or even running the six blocks. But she needed to give this some thought.

She quietly ate at dinner while her mind buzzed with planning for tomorrow. Her aloofness was normal for her of late, so it went unnoticed.

Mrs. Martin's office was a small study located at the foot of the steps leading up to the semi-private dormitory rooms. Off to one side of her office was her private quarters. She had a bedroom area, and an alcove furnished with a stuffed chair, ottoman, a reading lamp, and a bookcase. The office door was open, and Hattie could only see Mrs. Martin's hands as she sat writing at her desk. She knocked.

"Yes, who is there?" Mrs. Martin responded.

"It's Hattie Moore, Mrs. Martin. May I come in?"

"Yes, come in dear." Mrs. Martin called all unmarried women "Dear."

"Mrs. Martin. A messenger came today and left me a note from my father." Mrs. Martin knew an envelope had arrived but did not know who it was from. She nodded and gestured for her to continue. "Well, I'm very excited. Father will be in town tomorrow for only a few hours, while he attends to some business in town. He would like to meet me at Stanford's Luggage at one o'clock and then join him for lunch. I hope this isn't too inconvenient, I mean with such short notice and all. His train leaves promptly at three o'clock so he asked that I meet him there. I hope that you can find the time to accompany me."

Mrs. Martin pursed her lips as she evaluated what Hattie had said. Stanford's Luggage is where the most respected Texans shopped for luggage. Traditionally, when parents took their Wainwright-schooled daughters to Europe, their first stop would be Stanford's. Considering what a thorn Hattie had been, the school would be so much better off with her traveling in Europe with her parents. Since the shop was only two blocks away; Mrs. Martin didn't see any reason to break up her day to chaperone a child visiting her own father.

"Yes, you can go. And I will make an exception; you may go unaccompanied. Just be sure you return promptly after you've concluded your business."

"Thank you, Mrs. Martin."

Mrs. Martin's attention was already back to her writing. "Goodnight, dear."

"Goodnight Mrs. Martin."

The next day Hattie left the school at 11:45 and walked calmly towards the luggage store. When she knew she could no longer be seen, even from Wainwright's second-floor windows, she changed direction and hastened towards City Hall.

When Hattie arrived, Earl was sitting on a stone bench watching an elderly man feed the pigeons. Earl was wearing a dark blue suit one size too large for his frame, a shirt he had previously purchased with Hattie's father's money, and a bolo tie. He was dangling a small bouquet of daisies from his right hand.

"Earl!" she called out ahead.

He sprang up causing the small group of gray birds to scatter into the air. "Hattie!" he joyously called back.

They ran towards each other but stopped short of embracing. Earl was smiling from ear to ear. "Hattie, it's so good to see you."

"It's wonderful to see you, Earl. Why are you here? Why can't you stay longer?"

Earl's face turned serious. "Hattie" he said nervously, "I know this is going to come out of the blue, but I've got something very important to tell you." He then motioned her towards an unoccupied bench further away from the old man.

"Hattie, I've saved enough money, well almost enough, to homestead some land out in New Mexico. I can get a hundred and sixty acres from an agent out there, but he's transferring to another region in a couple of weeks. The land already has a working well and a house. Earl forgot to give Hattie the flowers and was waving the bouquet around in the air as he spoke. "Hattie, do you know what I'm saying?"

"I guess you're leaving. Are you here to say goodbye?"

"Well, I guess I am leaving, but I don't want to say goodbye. Hattie, will you come with me? I know we haven't had the proper amount of courtin' time, but will you marry me? Marry me now, today?" He was nervous and speaking rapidly. "I've got to get back to finish a job I was getting paid extra for. And I 've got to pay up on that wagon I put a deposit on and..." Hattie reached over and touched his cheek.

"Yes, Earl. I'll marry you today."

Earl stopped talking mid-sentence, looked into the face of his future bride, and handed her the half-broken bouquet of flowers.

After the quick ceremony at the Justice of the Peace, Hattie wired her parents. "Mother and Father, Earl Curtis and I have wed today. Taking next train to Amarillo. Love Hattie." The next

train would be at seven o'clock, just barely enough time for Hattie to get her things from the school and meet Earl at the station.

Mrs. Martin was shocked and angry, but there wasn't much she could or wanted to do about the situation. Hattie was a legally-married woman and there were plenty of girls on the waiting list and ready to take her spot at this prestigious school. She would make no attempt to persuade Hattie to stay.

When Hattie reached the station, the conductor was already calling "all aboard." Earl greeted her with a short kiss and a warm hug. Except the peck in front of the Justice of the Peace, this was the most physical contact they had since they met. "Well, here we go" Earl said and gestured in a wide sweeping motion to the stairs leading to the passenger car. Hattie smiled, took one suitcase while Earl gathered up the others. Hattie's girlhood dream of the West and adventure was about to come true.

Because Earl worked for the railroad he had free passage for himself and his wife. However, he did not hold a high enough position to garner a sleeping birth. Earl also knew he did not have enough money to purchase meals in the dining car. So, while Hattie was gathering her belongings at school, he purchased apples, peanuts, saltines, beef jerky, and a bag of hard candies to sustain them. For the next two days, they leaned against each other nodding off a few minutes at a time to the repetitious sounds of clack-a-ta-clack-a-ta and the echoes of the whistle ahead.

As the train approached the Amarillo station Earl and Hattie bickered about who would do the talking. Hattie thought it best if she did the explaining since she knew her father. Earl thought it best for him to do the talking because he felt it was his place as the head of his family.

At last, the engine slowly chuffed as the heavy steel wheels came to a stop at the platform. From behind a final cloud of engine steam, Mr. Moore stepped onto the platform and suddenly neither wanted to do the talking.

The newlyweds stepped down onto the passenger platform, and not knowing what else to do, placed their few bags on the ground. Mr. Moore signaled a man to step forward and gather up the luggage. It was Leroy.

Without a word, the family stepped up into the surrey. Leroy climbed in and snapped the reins. There was a jerk and the team pulled them on to the Moore's place.

After about ten minutes of silence, Mr. Moore looked at this daughter and asked "Tell me Hattie and tell me true. Did you have to get married? I mean would there be shame on the family if you didn't get married?" Quite surprisingly, he asked in a gentle quiet tone. He already had assumed the worst and hoped his daughter had not really gone astray.

Ever since the telegram arrived he cast blame on himself for letting his wife force Hattie into finishing school. He knew deep in his heart that she was wasn't the high society type, just the way he knew he wouldn't ever would quite fit. Also, his wife blamed him for letting Hattie get too close to the working class.

Mrs. Moore always felt she married beneath her station and loathed the times when she and Tyler had little to show for themselves. She never expected her children to want for any less than she wanted for herself. Now Tyler was looking for an answer from Hattie. Did he fail as a father?

"No Papa. There's nothing for anyone to feel ashamed about." Hattie hadn't called her father Papa since she was thirteen but saw the worry and hurt in his eyes. "I want so many of the same things that Earl wants; to make our own way, to take a piece of the West for ourselves the way you did Papa. Is that so bad? Mother may not agree, but I really tried. I'm not made for fine white gloves. I should be wearing leather work gloves right alongside my husband.

He took a large handkerchief out of his coat pocket, wiped his face like a wash cloth and blew his nose hard into the center of it. He cleared his throat a couple of times before trying to speak and took his daughter's hand into his.

"You know I always dreamed of the day I'd give my little girl away. Sometimes I'd think about how beautiful you would look and how proud I'd be walking you down the aisle. Then the next minute, I'd rile myself up just thinking about the cost of a fancy wedding; funny thing, this parenting business."

For the remainder of the trip, Hattie explained the necessity of haste and the plans they made. Mr. Moore listened intently and looked at Earl who occasionally nodded in agreement. In many ways, Hattie's father wished he could go with them, to start all over, to really feel alive.

The sun was going down by the time they arrived at the big house. Mrs. Moore's silhouette was peering out the parlor window and disappeared when the surrey came to a halt.

"Leroy, you take the luggage over to the guest house and take care of the rig." Mr. Moore got down and helped his daughter to the ground. Earl got out and stood on the other side of Hattie. Leroy gently snapped the reins and drove the rig behind the side of the house.

"Listen kids," Mr. Moore said." This isn't going to be easy." You go directly to the dining room and have yourself a good home-cooked meal. I'm sure where you're goin' a good meal will be far between. I'll have a talk with Mrs. Moore and we'll see you in the morning. I'll tell Cassie to send some dinner up to us later." He took a large breath like a man getting ready to jump naked into a cold stream. Hattie reached out to her father, kissed him on the cheek and whispered "Thank you, Papa. I love you." He smiled, turned, and walked into the house.

After Hattie and Earl were satisfied that her parents were upstairs, they went to the dining room. Within minutes, Cassie brought in heaping plates of chicken, sweet potatoes, cornbread, and a huge bowl of green beans with bacon. While there was a lot of emotion being vented somewhere upstairs, Earl and Hattie looked at each other in delight and ate like starved peasants.

Within three days, Earl and Hattie were ready to depart. As a wedding present Mr. Moore gave them two horses, a covered buckboard wagon, a plow, two shovels, two hoes, a post digger, carpenters' tools, rope, a well pump, an assortment of garden vegetable seeds, and two hundred dollars.

Mrs. Moore did some shopping while in town the day before. She planned to give the couple a fine lace tablecloth, matching napkins, and bone china. Fortunately, Cassie, who had accompanied her to town, heard her place the order and interceded.

"Mrs. Moore? Mrs. Moore, would you pardon me intruding in on you?" This was highly unusual on two counts. First, what was a black woman doing interrupting a conversation between two white people, and secondly, Cassie had never interrupted before. Because of this, Mrs. Moore excused herself from the clerk.

"I think it best if we could talk in private if you don't mind?" Cassie said discretely. "All right, then, let's step outside." Mrs. Moore called back to the clerk telling him she would return in a few minutes.

"Now Mrs. Moore, you know that my family been with your family for three generations. And you know there be plenty of times when we could have just got up and left. I sayin' all this because I think down deep you trust me, just as down deep I trust you too."

"Come on Cassie, what is it?"

"Remember when you first came out here with Mr. Moore? You wrote me and your mama 'bout how hard it was to cook with only a fry pan and a coffee pot. Now Mr. Moore he was too proud to let your folks buy you what you needed. But this fella

Earl, I think he wouldn't mind the family helping some. They already married and it's too late to undo. You know I loves that little girl too and I think, well I just think she needs the practical things that would make her life easier. Now I just think that all this marriage stuff flew in so fast that the crazy dust done blind you. I know that if you had the time, you would come to see what I see. Don't you?"

Mrs. Moore did not respond directly to Cassie, but instead turned and walked back into the store. She looked visibly disappointed when she said, "Mr. Parker, I need to change that order."

"Ma'am?" Cassie drew her attention away again. "What now Cassie?" She snapped, almost crying.

"You know, a couple of nice handkerchiefs and maybe a fine doily or two won't take much room. You always make the prettiest choices of those dainty things. I bet Miss Hattie would love to have something pretty she could just take out and look at every now and then, especially when times are hard." Mrs. Moore's face froze momentarily while she contemplated Cassie's recommendation. Then her expression changed from to determination. "Why yes, I can find a few suitable items for Hattie. Small things can be rather nice."

She turned back to her maid, "You take care of ordering whatever grossly-utilitarian things you think Hattie could use. I'll be back with my selection shortly."

Mrs. Moore returned with silk handkerchiefs, gold brocade doilies, an eight-by-ten-inch picture frame she could fill with a

photograph of the three of them taken last spring, and a mother of pearl comb, brush, and hand mirror. Cassie looked up at Mrs. Moore, "Those things will mean so much to her. I just know it."

On the thirty-minute trip back to the house, Mrs. Moore lamented about the past. "Cassie, it was so hard when we started out. It troubles me to see Hattie embarking on the same grueling journey I took. I was pretty, young, and so naïve. I knew nothing about having to 'make-do' or even making babies for that matter. And, mind you, I believed every word that young and handsome Mr. Tyler promised." She looked out across the wide prairie and chuckled to herself. "Well, I guess he made good, but Lord knows a pyramid could have been built in between the promise and the delivery."

Several miles passed in silence and then Cassie said, "Your mama hated to see you go. She cried for days after you left. You know she didn't write for months, but I know she thought about you all the time. Your daddy hated seein' your mama so troubled, but there wasn't a thing he could do to get her out of her rut. He jus' had to wait until she was good and ready to crawl out of that dark place in her mind."

"I didn't know that. She never told me. I just assumed she was ashamed of me marrying that, what did she call him, that fortune hunter."

"She should have. She should have just told you the truth; simple as that – the truth. Why is love so hard to be truthful about?

Chapter Three – Betting the Homestead

The night before they left Amarillo they found it hard to fall asleep. Hattie thought, "I'm going to be a pioneer," and was as excited as an overstimulated child but did her best to keep still. She figured Earl needed to be well rested to start the one hundred thirteen-mile journey to Tucumcari in the New Mexico Territory.

Earl turned over to his side and with the full moon casting a pale glow through the window, he could just make out his reflection in the vanity mirror. He was pleased with how things had lined up so far and how clever he was in acquiring his homestead. Oh, sure there was a well-practiced slight-of-hand maneuver, but if that bone-headed, would-be buckaroo was too dimwitted to catch it, well, he never should have tried to play with the big boys. Hell, when that Percy Beaumont joined the table he should have never gulped down those two whiskeys and he should've known better than to brag. Earl rolled back over on to his back and stared at the ceiling.

Percy foolishly boasted to the men at the table that his New Mexico homestead would be claimed up within a few weeks and, he just came to back to Amarillo to wed his fiancé who promised to marry him just as soon as he finally proofed up his stake.

Earl remembered how he cleverly ordered another drink for himself and yet another for Percy who must have felt he was on a winning streak.

When the drinks came Earl said, "Well Percy, at this rate you'll be able to afford some breeding done on your place...," he paused to look at the other men, "and maybe get a few animals too!" The men laughed, but Percy didn't get the joke.

As the cards were dealt again, Earl studied the man. Though Percy tried to keep a straight face, his eyes opened wide and his breathing changed. There was something going on in his head and he was doing some calculating. He glanced at his small pile of cash and frowned, which inadvertently signaled Earl that Percy was anticipating his big chance.

After a few bets around the table only Percy and Earl remained. Now it was Earl's big chance as well. He needed to bet much more than Percy was showing on the table to get what he really wanted, but would Percy bite?

Earl placed his cards face down as he continued to pretend he had over imbibed and couldn't straighten his cards out into a clean row. He gulped the rest of his drink and with slightly slurred speech he said, "I'm betting that you couldn't have a winning hand after the last two, the odds just aren't there. I think you're bluffing. Tell you what, I'll see your twenty and raise you fifty along with my prize horse and the custom-made saddle. All told, that's got to be over a hundred."

Percy took another look at his cards. It was a full house and this drunken cowboy looked a great deal more cocky than smart.

Percy sat up straight, "Tell you what. I'll beat that." He reached down into a leather satchel laying by his feet and pulled out a document. "This is my homestead. It has one hundred and sixty acres, got a good well, and a house."

Earl took a quick look at the document and replied, "But you said it won't be proofed up for a few more weeks; it's not yours to bet."

Percy stood up and smoothed the paper out on the table for everyone to see. The paper described the property and specified the homestead as being proofed up by Percy Beaumont as of a week ago.

Earl scratched his head, "Is this legal?"

"It is if you can move to New Mexico within the next few weeks with a hundred dollars in your hand."

Earl questioned, "How's that?"

"Look, the territory agent handling the homestead deeds in the area is Alfred Tutman and he's planning to move to Seattle by the first of November to start a business with his brother. He's made a lot of cash under the table by doing favors for folks. For a hundred dollars and a letter from me saying to make the title out to you, he'd be more than happy to oblige."

Just for show, Earl took another peek at his cards. "Tell you what, you write that letter now, and have two of these fine gentlemen witness it. We'll place it in the center of kitty along with this document, and I'll accept your bet; but you won't because you're bluffing."

One of the men got some paper and a pen from the bartender and as Percy penned the letter, Earl's mind raced ahead. He would finally have his own spread, and hell, a big portion of the work was already done.

He needed to figure out a way to get his hands on more cash. By payday he'd have just enough to pay off Tutman, but he needed a grubstake to get through the winter and to buy stock in early spring.

Percy stood up and displayed the letter to the room and then put it and the witnessed document on top of the kitty. "Call" he said, like a man twice his size and four times more experience. "I got a full house." Percy laid down his cards and without waiting for Earl to show his hand, started to grab for the pile."

"Now you just hold on there." Earl said in a calm voice. Suddenly there was nothing but the sound of a tobacco wad hitting the bottom of the brass spittoon in the far corner of the room. "You may have a full house, but my three Kings over deuces beats your what?"

A man overlooking Percy's shoulder said, "Tens over fours."

Chapter Four –
Finding Help

It was April 1905, and Hattie tugged at a stubborn clump of tangle-head weeds popping up in her fledgling vegetable garden. For the past two months, she fought a never-ending battle to get in a viable garden. But between the weeds, rabbits, her pregnancy, and the weather she was losing. She straightened up, took a rag from her pocket, and mopped away the dust and perspiration. Just last month she could barely keep warm from a late snowfall. Now at the end of April, the cloudless sky made the air punishingly hot.

No one from back home would recognize her. The radiant youthful girl that once captivated the young men at the ball had, over the past eight months, turned into a mere shadow of herself. Despite working daily under the sun her skin did not tan but remained pale and blotchy. She knew that she was no longer beautiful; she could tell by the way Earl avoided looking at her, and by the way she felt; drained.

Earl had told the truth when he said there was a house on the land. But it was built of shoddy materials by a man in a hurry. The high desert winter seeped in between the planks and where

the roof joined the eaves. They would have been better off living in the eight-by-eight-foot root cellar which once served as a small sod house for Percy Beaumont. Earl said that Percy's bride-to-be would not marry him if it meant living like a prairie dog, so Percy removed the sod-roof structure and built the existing house on top of it.

Throughout the winter months Earl obsessively rationed everything they had, especially firewood and food. Hattie was sure her father gave them enough staples and cash to get them through the first year. But Earl said he needed the money to start a real cattle herd and what they had wasn't enough, not nearly enough. In fact, whenever the subject of money came up he became angry and often stormed out of the house. Sometimes he would go to the barn and she could hear him throwing things around, while other times he would disappear into town.

She tried but couldn't understand his thinking. There were plenty of ranchers in the area starting out small; why couldn't he be happy to do the same?

Today she had only worked for thirty minutes but was already exhausted. She tried but could not keep up with the tasks she laid out for herself, or for that matter, for the past six months. She was determined that whatever reasons Earl had for brooding, she would not be the cause for any of it. She would keep up her end. She straightened her back and using her hoe for support made her way towards the next large clump of weeds.

Earl didn't know how long Hattie had been lying in the dirt. He did not panic and simply got down off his horse. His first thought was that at least the ground was soft where she fell. His second thought was that in her condition she probably needed a doctor. That was followed quickly by the thought that doctors cost money.

He wondered if they could wait to see if she got better on her own. Everyone knew that Dr. Pierce spent most of his time in town but would also ride out to make medical calls in neighboring Liberty and Melrose on Thursdays and Fridays. But today was Wednesday and if he did not take her into town today she would not be seen until Saturday. Damn, they had to go today.

Hattie was obviously too weak to sit up in the wagon seat, so Earl laid her down on a makeshift bed of straw in the back. Too tired to argue anymore about her unfinished work, she quietly took direction. As she lay there, the movement of the wheels over the uneven ruts swayed her back and forth like a cradle. The sun was warm and soon her exhausted body nodded off into a much-needed sleep.

Dr. Pierce's office was in his home. He had a wide screened-in porch where most patients waited to be seen, a parlor where they waited during inclement weather, and behind two large sliding doors, the formal dining room was converted into an examining room.

He did not have a nurse or an assistant but would call upon either the Methodist minister or the young Catholic priest, to lend a hand when needed. This worked out very well since his white patients did not trust the Mexican priest, and his Mexican patients always felt reassured with the Father in the room should *The Lord Our Father* call during surgery. He occasionally called on Rosalinda, though he knew her stepfather demanded all her wages. But Dr. Pierce always managed to slip her a little cash on the side.

The short nap did Hattie some good and she felt well enough to walk into the house. Although she leaned heavily on Earl's arm, she negotiated the few steps leading into the doctor's office. Dr. Pierce instructed Hattie to step up and sit on his examining table, which she managed as if she were an eighty-year-old woman. Earl looked the doctor over to try to get a sense of the man, though he was the only doctor within sixty miles. He was in his late fifties, slightly shorter than average, and lean of build. His face was delicate though sported a thick brown mustache contrasted by a pronounced receding hairline. His clear blue eyes, magnified through his rimless spectacles, conveyed a focus well suited for a physician. Earl thought he looked too smart and probably uppity. If he were to meet him in the street, he would not make an effort to say hello.

The doctor checked for fever, peered into her throat, and gently pushed her upper and lower eyelids back. He moved his fingers down to her neck, softly pushing the tissue below her ears and under her jaws. He then examined the color of her fingernails, turned her hands over and moved his thumb over her calluses. He then removed her shoes and felt around both ankles.

While he methodically moved from one part of her body to the other, he asked, "Have you had any problems passing water?"

"No. In fact, I've had to go more often than usual," Hattie replied.

"Any pain or discomfort when you go?"

"No, just a little burning sensation."

"How has your back been feeling?"

Hattie hesitated. She didn't want Earl to know she had been keeping her problems to herself, but mostly she did not want him to think she could not do her share of work.

"It's been mostly all right. Every now and then I've got to sit down for a minute. But it always passes."

"How long ago did you start getting these pains?"

"About three weeks ago."

"Any vomiting?"

"Sometimes."

He gave a little sigh and then pulled a large amber bottle from the shelf. Earl and Hattie watched as he carefully measured fifteen spoonsful of powder into a smaller bottle. Then he wrote something on the blank label, corked the top and handed it to Earl.

"Can you read?"

"Yes, better than most." Earl snipped.

Dr. Pierce wasn't so sure, so he told him the instructions any way, "One teaspoon in a glass of water, then drink while effervescent." He paused, and then added "while it's still bubbling."

The five days of the medication was bad enough, but the long-term treatment was the most difficult to hear.

Dr. Pierce put his hands on his hips and looked at Hattie. "Eat plenty of fresh meat, fruit, vegetables, milk, and most of all, stay in bed."

Unfortunately, their budget dictated beans, salt pork, corn meal, coffee, and a good helping and a half of hard work for the two for them. Earl could take care of the ranch work, but it was painfully obvious they needed help with the women's work.

The doctor suggested that Earl talk with his housekeeper's husband Reynaldo Garcia, to inquire if his wife, Teresa, or perhaps one of his sisters-in-law would be available. It would only be for a few weeks until Hattie just needed part-time assistance. Earl reluctantly nodded in acceptance and got directions to the Garcia home. Meanwhile, Hattie was told to rest awhile longer in the doctor's parlor.

She felt angry with herself for being so weak, but too weak to spend the energy to remain angry. In a short time, she was dozing off again.

After turning off the main street, Earl found himself in the Mexican part of town. His presence caught the attention of everyone in sight. Each person's gaze followed him as he moved further into their territory. Whenever a white man came into the area, which was rare, it was usually to accuse one of the residents of some wrong doing, some encroachment, or some unpleasantness that needed a swift solution. So, what ill fate was this man bringing? Their eyes followed him. Who would be picked out this time?

Earl became increasingly tense as the sounds of Main Street shrank into muffles behind him. It was not a hot day, but he felt the sweat forming under his leather hat band. A few years back he worked with Mexican cowboys on a spread near the border and marveled at their skills with a rope and riding. One of them even offered to show him how to jump through a twirling lariat. However, he felt threatened whenever there was more than one.

He never understood why they stayed on the American side of the border when they should have packed up and headed south to be with their own kind. Like previous tenants on foreclosed land, Earl thought they should have had the decency to leave. But for now, he had to put those thoughts aside. No white woman could possibly spare the time away from her own family so like it or not he would have to make do.

Mr. Garcia was already standing in his doorway by the time Earl figured out which structure he should approach.

It was difficult to tell how old Reynaldo was. His voice was as clear and strong as a thirty-year-old, but he was missing two

upper left teeth and his skin was hard and weathered. He made his living making forms for adobe bricks but spent the majority of his time laying them.

"Are you Reynaldo Garcia?" Earl asked.

"Si, yes I am Reynaldo Garcia," the man answered.

"My name is Curtis. Earl Curtis. Dr. Pierce thought that you might be able to help me out with a little problem. I'll pay for the help. I don't have much, but I'll pay." Earl wanted Reynaldo to know right off that he wasn't asking for any favors.

"What kind of help are you looking for? Do you need a wall?"

"Actually, it's my wife. She's expecting in about a month and well, she's not doing very good. The doctor says he thinks she's just run down pretty bad. She's supposed to stay in bed for a few weeks and then just ease back into her regular work when she's up to it. Doc Pierce thought that your wife or maybe one of her sisters might be able to help tend to her."

"*Para que*? Err, how much you pay?"

Earl had to think quickly, he hadn't even thought about it." "I'll pay room and board and fifty cents a day. She's got to be able to take on all the chores Hattie, my wife, was doin' before she got sick."

Reynaldo nodded, indicating he understood what Earl was saying. He held up one finger gesturing that he would be back in a moment and disappeared into the house.

Earl heard talking between Reynaldo and a woman in Spanish. He did not understand what they were saying, but Earl could tell that the woman disagreed. The tone of the conversation worried Earl and he anxiously waited for Reynaldo to come back with an answer.

When Reynaldo returned he ordered Earl to "come." "We will go to see my niece at my brother Hector's house." Earl did not ask what happened in the house but knew it would be best to follow Reynaldo.

They walked still further away from town until they turned at a bend. A breeze kicked up road dust as they walked in silence. In a few minutes they arrived at a small adobe house. An acre of corn, and another well-tended acre of assorted produce was planted behind it. On the east side there was a dilapidated corral for two milking goats and about a dozen chickens milling about the yard, casually pecking at the ground. Off to the west stood an equally dilapidated shed.

Suddenly, a large dog darted towards them from behind the house. He was barking insanely, ears flattened, snorting in the dusty air as he ran. His powerful legs kicked up dirt and scattered the chickens into hiding with each stride. Earl anxiously reached down for some rocks. When he looked up he could now see the dog's lips curled up over his teeth. A bullwhip cracked in the air like a gunshot and the dog jumped aside and sat cowering. Crack! The whip snapped again, and the dog cringed and then retreated in a near crawl to the back of the house.

The man with the whip, Hector, exploded into laughter watching the dog disappear. He then looked at Earl's blanched face and continued to laugh uncontrollably. He would point in the direction of the dog laughing, then point at Earl's face and laugh some more.

Reynaldo was not so amused by Hector as he unsuccessfully tried to show him the humor in it all. He finally started to calm down and wiped his eyes with his shirt sleeve. Earl quickly sized him up as a slothful man. He was fat in the face and hands, and the dirt on his clothes was likely from laziness not from ranch sweat and soil.

Reynaldo, speaking in Spanish, explained what Earl wanted. He then added that his commission should be half of the two weeks' salary. At this point Hector started shouting at Reynaldo; Earl could not understand the words, but easily interpreted the vulgar gesture. As he ranted on, his round oily jowls reminded Earl of a pig's behind.

Hector then turned to Earl and said, "Follow me."

They walked to a shed and stepped in with Reynaldo lagging behind. The unkempt chicken coop had an acrid odor, but the fowl inside were not laying hens. Hector took a tin cup off a nail and reaching into a wooded barrel scooped up a cup of grain. He then carefully filled the bowls set in the individual cages. He talked as he went about doing this for each of the six cages.

"So, my name is Hector. I am Reynaldo's older brother. He likes to try to pull a fast one on me because he is taller, but you and I talk now. He says your esposa, uh wife, is sick with the

baby. You want for somebody to do the work and stay with her. Is this right?"

"Yes, that's about it."

Hector pulled down one of the cages for closer examination. It was a magnificent fighting cock. Earl got closer to the other cages and saw five other impressive animals.

"These sure look like winners." Earl said to Hector.

"Do you know about the cock fighting?"

"No, not really. Once when I was a hired hand up in the panhandle, the boys thought I should see one. The fight just got to goin', and money was flying hand to hand when the place caught fire. We all got out, but that was the end of that. I do know one thing, your roosters you got here look a hell of a sight better than the ones they had."

Hector took in the compliment, nodded, and returned the cage to finish filling the other cups with feed. They stepped back outside, and Earl was glad to breathe the fresh air.

"I have two daughters who are not yet married. The young one, Cecelia, is my bonita, very pretty, and can get a husband easy. She will stay here so I can watch what she does and who will come. I will choose when it is time and who she will marry. Not for a day do I leave my Cecelia alone. Now Rosalinda…" he paused, "only the dog thinks she is beautiful." He laughed cruelly and then spat on the ground. "You can take her, but you will pay me. I will take half a dollar now."

"I think that I should at least see her before saying it's a deal." Earl knew he really didn't have a choice but wanted it to appear like he had some control.

"Si, I will fetch her." Hector responded and went into the house.

It has been over forty-five minutes since Earl left the doctor's office and he was anxious to get back to town. He watched a lizard dart around the edges of the wall and could hear the muffled sounds of arguing. The woman's arguing came to an abrupt halt with the sound of a slap. Hector came out and a few seconds later a woman, who appeared to be in her early twenties, walked out behind him. From several feet away, Earl could see a fresh red mark across her right cheek the size of a flapjack.

"This is Rosalinda. Ask her what you want."

Earl thought for a second. "Do you speak English?"

"Yes, I can speak English." She spoke with surprising clarity, much better than her father.

"Good. My name is Earl Curtis. My wife's sick and needs tending to, and her chores need doin' too. Got any trouble with that?"

"I tended to my mother's injuries and did her work and mine. No, that won't trouble me. Sometimes I help Dr. Pierce."

"Where's your mother now?"

Hector jumped in, "That's all now. You want her or not? I am a busy man. Well?"

"Goddamn typical Mexicans," he thought to himself. He reached into his pants pocket, jerked out a fifty-cent piece, and gave it to Hector. "Here."

Turning to Rosalinda he continued, "I'm headin' back to see the doctor. Just take what you can carry for now. We've got to go."

Hector butted in. "You take the dog with you."

"Wait a minute. Wait a goddamned minute. We never talked about no goddamn blood-thirsty dog." The veins on his neck and forehead began to bulge. "That dog ought to be shot. He's going to kill someone, and it sure ain't gonna be me. You people really got the goddamn gall."

Reynaldo, who walked over to the shed, started to slip his hand towards a pitch fork leaning against the rain barrel.

Rosalinda raised her voice. "Mr. Curtis, he won't hurt you. I promise. Shakespeare won't hurt you. He'll keep the coyotes away from your livestock and crows away from your corn."

Earl did a double take at the dog's name. But by now he was totally frustrated and confused – he needed to get back into town. "Look, if he even growls at me I got the right to shoot him." He turned towards Reynaldo. "Comprehende? I'll shoot him." He turned back again to Rosalinda "I'll shoot him." Earl paused and took a breath. "You go on in and get your stuff. I'll wait for you up the road there on that rock. Hurry up now."

Earl was done talking. He turned and started walking back the way they came. Hector walked over towards Reynaldo by the shed and they laughed at who knows what.

When Earl got to the rock he sat down and sighed in emotional exhaustion. Every muscle in his body was tight, wound up like a new roll of barbed wire. He rubbed the back of his neck but found little relief.

After about ten minutes, Rosalinda was in sight. She had a large bundle in what looked like a tablecloth fashioned into a sling-like sack hanging down on her right side and pulled to a knot on top of her left shoulder. From her left hand, Shakespeare trotted to her side on a short length of rope.

Fearing that the dog would make chase, Earl gathered a few more egg-size stones, ready to throw them.

Soon Rosalinda and the dog stood in front of him. Shakespeare sat and gave his neck a scratch with his hind foot, seeming to care less about the man in front of him. Earl was not reassured, so he stuffed the stones into his pocket.

There were no words. They just walked at a steady pace back to town.

Chapter Five – Picking Stones from Your Heart

Dr. Pierce was sitting outside on the front steps enjoying a smoke. Unless an emergency came in, he figured that he was done for the day. Besides Hattie, he had tended to one broken arm caused by Cal Perkins' not quite so broken-in horse; an infected wound on a foot that started out as a blister that Gil Bennett just couldn't see going to the doctor for earlier; and the four Lester children who had fevers and coughs. He dragged the cigarette smoke in deeply and blew it out slowly like pouring molasses over pancakes.

When he was a young doctor in Chicago he had a thriving office, making a very good living. He figured out very early that the more patients he saw in a day, the more money he earned. The more money he earned the more respect he received from his peers.

He had loved that life of being a god until he found he wasn't. It is true what they say, "Pride cometh before the fall." His fall came in the form of a bad prescription causing a nine-year-old girl to go blind. There was no trial, no inquisition. The girl's parents were in awe of him and he lied about the cause. He told them it was extremely rare for her illness to progress into blindness, but it did happen occasionally. In fact, only he knew that her illness never would have progressed into blindness.

49

He drank heavily for months on end trying to dull his guilt. He rarely saw patients, causing deep financial stress. His colleagues never asked him about his troubles; they simply aligned themselves with a brighter rising star. It didn't take long for Dr. Pierce to acknowledge that there wasn't anything about himself that he liked or wanted to be around.

Several months had passed when he happened to be drinking down his lunch a block away from his room. He had seen it dozens of times, but he never really looked at it. He squinted his sore eyes to focus on a framed picture of Doc Holiday hanging over the cash register. It was raining outside, and the drops streaking down the bar's window cast eerie trailing shadows against it. He had been staring at it for a good thirty minutes when the bartender asked him if he ever dreamed of being a cowboy. "Yeah, right," he sarcastically replied and downed the rest of the glass. He picked up his change, left a tip, and walked out into the rain. After a few steps, he stopped and asked himself, "what the hell, why not?"

He packed two suitcases, one for his clothes, and the other for his books and equipment. By three o'clock, he was on the train platform waiting to go southwest.

It took ten years for him to slowly make peace with his past. He traveled great lonely distances between insignificant towns seeing a few patients than making the long circle back. Somewhere between the years and the unending horizons, he learned to accept his burden just enough to live with himself.

Now he had found contentment seeing a half a dozen or patients on a good day and smoking a good cigarette.

Looking down the street, he saw Earl accompanied by a woman and a dog. "Well, one last piece of business for the day," he thought to himself, took one more puff and smashed the butt on the ground.

Earl told Rosalinda to wait by the wagon as he walked towards the doctor.

"I see you snagged Rosalinda. Good choice."

"You know her?"

"Yes, I do. Both she and her mother would help translate for me and assist me in nursing tasks now and then. Your wife's been doing fine this afternoon. She had a good meal and napped for a while."

"Good, I'm glad something's working out today."

"You still need to buy some nutritious food before you leave town. Best go in to say hello, and then get yourself over to Hatcher's store."

"Yeah, there's no rest for the weary." Earl answered and went in the house.

The doctor then walked over to Rosalinda. He could see some redness on one side of her face. "Has it been bad?"

"You know my stepfather. It's only bad when he's awake."

"I hope this works out for you, even if it's temporary."

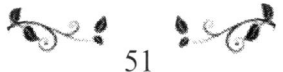

"I hope so too."

They spent the next couple of minutes talking about Mrs. Curtis' condition and the type of care she would need.

Earl came back outside. "I'll be back in a few minutes."

"Wait, why don't you take Rosalinda, she knows what to get and won't try to make you buy something you don't need."

Earl hesitated for a moment. "OK, she can go. The dog stays here."

"Dr. Pierce?" Rosalinda asked, "Do you have any scraps for Shakespeare? I didn't have a chance to feed him today."

"I probably do. Yes, I'm sure I do. I'll have it ready by the time you get back."

"For God's sake, let's go!" Earl barked.

"Thank you very much, Doctor."

When Earl and Rosalinda walked away, Dr. Pierce went over to the dog. He squatted down to the dog's eye level and scratched him behind the ear.

"Well, Shakespeare, haven't seen you in a bit. You look a tad on the lean side." The dog's large brown eyes smiled into his. He knew this man making noises with his mouth was a good man. "Are all the wild rabbits gone at your place? Come on back with me, we'll get you fixed up."

Shakespeare was on the back porch drinking from a pan of water while the doctor scrounged around in his pantry. "This should work," the doctor said. Into a large mixing bowl, he poured his last half a cup of milk, left-over cornbread, some bacon grease kept on the stove, and for good measure cracked two fresh eggs into the whole thing. He brought out the concoction, placed it in front of the dog, and watched him take in huge bites. Content that the dog would eat his fare, the doctor lit another cigarette.

Rosalinda knew the store so well she quickly found everything the doctor suggested and placed the items on the counter. Earl looked over everything and nodded acceptance.

"Will that be all?" Mr. Hatcher asked.

"I hope so. Yes, yes that's all," Earl replied.

As Mr. Hatcher added up the bill, Rosalinda stared into the candy jar of lemon drops. Her mouth was already watering just imagining the granules of sweet sugar melting into sourness on her tongue.

Mr. Hatcher looked up and saw her gazing at the container. "Can I fetch a couple out for you today, Rosalinda?" She was about to speak.

"This here alone is going to put me into debt more than I want. No one's getting' any candy."

Rosalinda reached into her pocket and pulled out a knotted handkerchief. Inside was a small handful of coins; she pulled out two cents and placed them on the counter. "When you're done with Mr. Curtis, I'll take two cents worth."

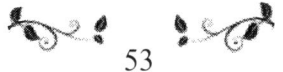

The totaled bill was handed over to Earl. "I want to pay this down some with what I got. I'll have to put the rest on my tab. Is that all right with you?" Earl and Hattie always paid off their small balances, so Mr. Hatcher had no problem with the arrangement.

Earl reached into his left pocket and pulled out three dollars, "Wait, I got a little more here." When he quickly yanked out the contents of his right pocket out tumbled twelve cents and several rocks.

"I can take an additional twelve cents off your bill, but I'm afraid I don't know the goin' rate for rocks."

"It's a long story and I'm short on time. I'd appreciate it if you got a box back there to haul this stuff."

Mr. Hatcher pulled a wooden produce box from behind the counter and gave it to Earl to load up. He then turned his attention to Rosalinda. "That was two cents worth, right?"

Rosalinda nodded and smiled as Mr. Hatcher rolled a small piece of brown wrapping paper into the shape of a cone, and then carefully folded up the bottom. He took a small metal scoop from another candy jar and scooped eight pieces into the little paper bag. He then folded the top down, just as he had done for her for the last fifteen years and handed it over the counter. Earl, watching from the corner of his eye, thought the portion seemed a lot for two cents, but didn't say anything.

"There you go, young lady. Hope to see you again soon."

"Thank you, Mr. Hatcher. Tell Mrs. Hatcher I said hello."

Earl had finished packing the groceries and signaled his head towards the door. Rosalinda opened it for Earl and then closed it behind them.

When they returned, Earl placed the groceries in the wagon and immediately walked into the doctor's house to get Hattie. Rosalinda noticed that Shakespeare wasn't where she tied him and started looking for him, calling out his name.

Dr. Pierce walked from around the back of his house. "I got him. Don't worry." He had the dog in tow and was carrying two flour sacks full of items. Rosalinda walked back to meet him.

"I decided to go ahead and feed him, so you wouldn't have to do it later on. I suppose you'll be pretty busy this evening settling in. Here's a sack of stuff for the dog. I had large tin of hardtack that a patient gave to me. I've had it for six months and I know I'll never eat it. Also, there are a couple of pounds of cornmeal in a tin. There're some weevils growing in there and I was about to throw it out anyway. Put the tin on the stove for a few minutes to kill the critters and it should be just fine for 'ol Shakespeare here. And, believe it or not, a crazy miner gave me several dozen dried squirrels. He said he figured out how to make jerky out of the things and eats them all the time. He wouldn't let me go without taking a whole bag full of them. Nutritionally speaking, if you chop one of those up into the rest of his food, I guess he'd be better for it. Funny, I just never know what I'll get for payment." He smiled then placed the two bags in the back corner of the wagon bed.

"Thank you, doctor. You've always been kind to us."

The screen door opened, and Earl came out with Hattie leaning heavily on his arm. She squinted from the orange glare even though the sun was low on the horizon. The doctor walked over, took Hattie's other arm, and the three shuffled over to the wagon. The two men lifted Hattie into the wagon bed and Earl jumped inside to position her for the trip home.

Rosalinda didn't know what, if anything, Earl or the doctor had told Hattie about herself. So, she just looked on, waiting for clues for what she should do next.

Earl climbed over the top to the seat and grabbed the reins. "See you in two weeks then," he called down to the doctor and then flipped the reins.

The wagon lunged forward leaving Rosalinda and her dog to follow on foot. At first the wagon pulled at a normal walking pace, but the horses, sensing they were on their way home, picked up some speed. Dust was now being kicked up from the wheels and carried by the wind into Rosalinda's face. The flying dust caused her to choke so she grabbed the light shawl from her head and wrapped it around her nose and mouth.

Hattie, who had dozed off momentarily, woke up just in time to see the girl stumble and fall behind the wagon. At first, she thought she was dreaming, but refocused her eyes. "Stop," she said, but she was barely audible. "Stop." This time she could almost be heard. "Stop. Earl, stop!" she yelled.

Earl yanked hard on the lines, set the brake, and jumped into the back with Hattie. "Hattie what's wrong? Where does it hurt?" Hattie was shaking her head, no.

"Back there – girl back there – she fell."

"What the...damn. I thought she was in the wagon." "Hold on, damn."

Rosalinda stood up, brushed herself off, and then walked towards them. As she reached them, Earl said, "Come on. Get in. Tie the dog to the end here, if you want." He didn't apologize or provide an excuse. He climbed back into the seat and held the reins. He impatiently waited for Rosalinda to settle in while resenting her for making him look foolish.

Rosalinda opted to let Shakespeare follow un-tethered, though Earl frowned at the sight of the untied dog. She sat across from Hattie, who had already started to doze off. Earl snapped the reins lightly and the rig was moving again. Shakespeare trotted along slightly off to the side, easily keeping up with the light pace. Rosalinda began to relax, stretching her legs out in front of her with her back resting against the side planks.

Nearly dozing herself, she looked at the woman across from her wondering what to expect. Would she be demanding or a tyrant? Would she demand frivolous attention, expecting her to be her hand maiden? Rosalinda imagined her ordering, "Get my mirror, get my handkerchief, and wipe my nose" to which she also imagined replying "Kiss my ass!" She continued staring at the sleeping woman's pale face. Maybe she's witless, the helpless type, or spineless, an empty, uninspired bore. She looked down at the woman's hands. There were no scars. They were tan but not leathery, and her nails were short but shaped. She looked again at the woman's face. She couldn't be over twenty, and there were no lines of bitterness in the corners of her mouth, tell-tailing a life of hardship. Why was she here? Did she run out of choices?

Twilight brought a familiar chill to these high plains, and the shadows stretched long below the mesas. Rosalinda untied her cloth bundle, brought out a serape, and pulled it over her head and shoulders. She glanced at Hattie and saw that she was asleep but was holding her arms together to retain heat. Seeing a blanket under Earl's seat, she pulled it out and gently placed it over Mrs. Curtis. After a few minutes, the moon was up bright, and fully illuminating the trail northwest to the homestead.

Rosalinda checked on Shakespeare and found that he was contently trotting along at the same pace. Satisfied, she folded herself under the serape and closed her eyes.

Earl maneuvered the team within a couple of yards of the house and came to a stop. Rosalinda, already awakened by the slowed gait of the team, sat up while Hattie remained asleep. As Earl tied the horses, Rosalinda stepped down onto the ground and patted her dog. She then led him over to a nearby trough where he took in great laps of cool water. When he finished he calmly sat down next to her, waiting for his queue.

For a few moments, Rosalinda just observed as Earl climbed into the back of the wagon to awaken his sleeping wife. Soon she

saw the woman slowly lift herself into a sitting position, was assisted up to stand, and then moved with Earl to the end of the wagon. Rosalinda moved to the opposite side of Earl to help support Hattie's weight as she searched for footing. Rosalinda gently picked up Hattie's left arm and placed it over her shoulder, then wrapped her own arm around her very thin waist. The sick woman was too groggy to notice the strange woman, concentrating only on making it into the house.

Rosalinda thought it peculiar that Earl, a seemingly strong man, simply didn't carry his wife in. She was, after all, very underweight... maybe he knew, she thought, that the woman had a fierce stubborn streak and would object, or maybe it simply did not occur to him. Certainly, it was not her place to suggest anything.

Once they got her into the bedroom, Rosalinda returned to the wagon to retrieve the groceries and supplies. With each trip she gave Shakespeare an assuring pat on the head. After several trips she turned to the dog and said, "I've got to find you a longer rope, but it might not be until tomorrow." She led him up onto the planked wooden porch and signaled him to lie down beneath the light of the window. "I'll come out when I can." She waited for him to make his routine circle and lay down, and then went back inside.

There wasn't much of anything on the kitchen shelves so making decisions on where to place things was easy. But before getting too involved, she decided to put together a quick dinner.

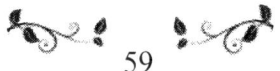

Fortunately, she had planned ahead and brought ingredients for a hearty bean soup made from canned red beans, canned tomatoes, fresh onions, rice, and ground chili. As the beans came to a slow rolling boil, she warmed tortillas directly on a flat open space on the surface of the stove. She felt lucky because every Wednesday, Mr. Hatcher sold fresh tortillas made by her elderly neighbor Melena. It was a welcome bit of home under a stranger's roof. Within a few minutes, the soup was ready, along with a fresh warm stack of tortillas, now keeping warm between a plate and an over-turned bowl.

She was hungry but would wait to eat. She set the pot back to a cooler part of the stove, ladled out a bowl, and set two folded tortillas across the brim. Carrying the dinner, she walked the few steps over to the bedroom and stood outside the open door.

"Mr. Curtis, I have some dinner for Mrs. Curtis. May I come in?"

"Yes, come in," he flatly responded.

She entered the small colorless room. There was a small square table next to the bed holding a tarnished oil lamp. A large cedar chest covered by a folded brown wool blanket sat at the foot of the bed. Along the walls were several rows of pegs to hang their wardrobes and on the far wall, a single curtainless window.

Hattie was sitting up and appeared a little more alert than half an hour earlier. While Rosalinda had tended to dinner, Earl had washed his wife's face and helped her into her bed clothes. Stepping closer to the bed she said "Hello, I'm Rosalinda. I have some dinner for you." She moved the lamp to make room for the bowl.

Hattie reached her hand out towards the bowl on the table.

"Here, let me help you a little." Rosalinda folded up a small flour sack towel, placed it on Hattie's lap, and then gently placed the bowl of soup on top of it. "There, I think you can handle it fine now, don't you?"

"Yes, this is much better." Hattie carefully filled her spoon, then gently blew across it before putting it into her mouth. She blew on the second spoonful but swallowed it much quicker than the first. She continued eating until she was almost half done. "This is very good," she said, barely looking up. She was so weak she could barely communicate anything more than the basics.

Rosalinda smiled, "Have some tortillas. I like to roll them up and dip them in the soup," she said while demonstrating how to roll the tortillas and dip them into an imaginary bowl.

"I've heard about tortillas, but never tried them," she said as she struggled a bit to roll the bread-like thing. Seeing her struggle, Rosalinda gently took the tortilla from her, rolled it, and placed it back in her hand. Hattie barely dipped the end into the soup then nibbled the wet end.

"You're trying to be too dainty, but maybe it's because you're still weak from the trip," she said trying to make her feel more at ease. "If you can, dunk it down about an inch and soak it up good. Some people don't even bother using a spoon if they have tortillas."

"Well, I hate being called dainty," she exclaimed and dipped the rolled tortilla deep into the tasty broth. This time she brought it up to her mouth and took a full bite. She smiled with inner delight as she chewed. It tasted and felt wonderful and she wished she was well enough to truly enjoy it.

Rosalinda watched as her student successfully finished her meal. "You did pretty good for it being the first time. Most people leave half of it on their chest." Hattie looked up. It was obvious that what she needed now was sleep, but Rosalinda asked, "Can I bring you anything more – more soup or tortillas?"

"No thank you," she responded, lifting the empty bowl up to Rosalinda. "I hope there's enough for Earl."

"Yes, I made enough for everyone." Hattie moved down into the bed while Rosalinda positioned the pillow with her free hand.

"Did you say your name was Rosalinda?" her eyes half closing as she spoke. "Pretty name," she yawned. "My name is Hattie, not as pretty; call me Hattie." For a second, she was silent, but in a moment just before falling asleep, she took a small breath and asked, "did you fall on your face?"

Rosalinda didn't bother answering. The woman was now definitely asleep. She gazed at her for a moment noticing the soft curve of her eyebrows and the slight dimple in her chin. Her face showed signs of being in the wind and sun for too long, too fast. This certainly was not a face weathered by long years in the field. She dimmed the lamp to a soft amber glow and pulled the covers up under Hattie's chin.

Rosalinda was hungry but decided that it would be presumptuous of her to sit down and eat before Earl, so she nibbled on a tortilla while she put the rest of the groceries up on the shelves.

When she finished, Earl still had not returned to the house. Partially out of curiosity, but mainly because of her growling stomach, she went out to see if she could lend him a hand. She found him in the small barn hanging up the team's reins. He heard her enter and only glanced at her while he worked.

"Mrs. Curtis ate all her dinner and is sleeping. Do you need some help; I mean is there something I can help you with out here?" She carefully corrected herself. Some men get very touchy when someone implies they "need help;" wanting and needing help were two different things.

"No, I'd say I'm about done," he said, hoisting a large sack of grain onto a table.

Rosalinda quickly scanned the interior of the barn. To the left side of the floor she spotted what appeared to be several feet of clothesline. "Would you mind if I borrowed that line on the floor to tie up Shakespeare for the night?"

Earl hadn't noticed the clothesline before and didn't immediately know what she was talking about or where to look. "Oh that. Go ahead. The last thing I want is that animal loose around here," he said walking out the door.

She quickly walked over to the pile and snatched it up while Earl waited outside the door until she came out. When she emerged, he latched the wooden doors. "Oh, I forgot," Earl said and disappeared back into the barn.

He returned carrying a bundle of something made of wood and canvas. "This a cot that was left behind by the first people who were here. I'll get it set up for you in the house." There was no kindness in his voice, just statement of fact. He could have just as well been talking to the wagon. "Here's your wheel. I'll put it on for you."

Rosalinda had been so busy since their arrival that she hadn't even thought about where she was going to sleep. She looked at the bundle and was glad she wouldn't be sleeping on the floor or in the barn.

Rosalinda served up two bowls of bean soup and warmed a few tortillas while Earl checked on Hattie. A moment later he returned. "She's still asleep," he said while pulling out his chair. He looked up realizing she was getting ready to place her bowl on the table. "Listen, no offense, but I'd like it better if you'd take your supper when I'm through. We're not friends and you're not family. I'd just as soon eat alone." By the look on her face, he could tell that his words came across more sharply than intended. He then quickly added, "I got a lot to think about."

Rosalinda calmly picked up her food and went outside. She placed the bowl and tortillas on the wooden bench and went over to Shakespeare. She gave him a scratch behind the ear and then tied the longer length of rope to his short lead. "There you go,

boy." He waited a couple of seconds to be sure she was finished with whatever she wanted to do, then disappeared around the corner to relieve himself and explore his new surroundings.

She sat on the bench thinking that she actually preferred eating alone as well. Soon she heard Earl finish off the last of the soup. That was good, at least she wouldn't be blamed for cooking more than would be eaten in one sitting. Waste was rarely tolerated by anyone she knew.

Shakespeare returned to her side wanting attention. "You're a good dog. This won't be so bad," she said and leaned up against the house. The moon was now high in the night sky, shining bright enough to cast soft shadows. Miles away coyotes began crying out in search of one another. "Well, at least we know where we are, and we're together," she said scratching under his chin.

A ripped horse blanket was crumpled up on top of a wooden crate next to the bench. Rosalinda got up for a closer look and saw that the crate was open on one side. "This should work nicely, I think," she said to the dog. "Come on; let's see how you like it. Come on." She pointed to the inside of the crate and Shakespeare dutifully got in and lay down. Rosalinda then draped the blanket over the open end and secured it with two heavy rocks. She scrunched down and pulled the flap over to the side. "This is the best I can do for now. I'll see you in the morning."

After she felt sure Earl was done eating, she went in to wash the bowls and the pot. She then refilled the pot with water and set it on the table. Then she poured several cups of dried pinto beans into a metal dish. Grabbing a handful of beans at a time, she picked out the stones and dropped the beans into the pan of water, repeating the process until the metal bowl was empty. She always liked doing this just before going to sleep, as did her mother, who once told her, "If you pick the little stones out of the beans before you go to sleep, you also pick out the little stones you gathered up in your heart during the day. This way your heart won't be as heavy when you get up in the morning." She never could pick out enough stones to lighten her heart, but enjoyed the moment remembering one of her mother's little sayings.

The house was still as she quietly placed a lid on the pot, wiped the bowls, and placed them on the shelf.

Earl hadn't thought to show her how to set up the cot, but she soon figured out how to put it together. Luckily, the bundle contained a small wool blanket, so she could roll her serape up into a pillow. She heard snoring from the other room and finally began to relax. She turned down the oil lamp and waited until the flame faded out before lying down. The moon seemed even brighter than earlier. It cast enough light through the window for her to make out the pot of beans soaking on the table. There was much to think about, but she could not muster the energy to stay awake.

Chapter Six –
Where's Earl?

Rosalinda awoke to her own natural alarm clock at four o'clock. Looking out the window, she saw that the moon was now on the opposite side of the evening sky and about to disappear behind the western hills. She stood, quietly slipping on her shoes, and unrolling her serape to wear. She then reached into her cloth bag and found her brush, soap, and a toothbrush.

Except for the moonlight, the sky was nearly black as she walked outside, placing her items on the crate. Hearing her come out, Shakespeare poked his head out of the crate.

"Hi boy, how'd you sleep?" she whispered. "I'll be back in a minute."

He intently watched her as she stepped quickly to the outhouse and continued until she returned a few minutes later.

The chilly air nipped at her skin, but Rosalinda felt it best to wash up and comb her hair away from the occupants of the house. Also, maintaining some degree of privacy helped her feel more in control, less vulnerable. She gave the pump handle a few good pumps and soon water gushed into the hanging bucket. Being careful not to splash water on herself, she rinsed and patted her face dry with a corner of her serape. Shakespeare moved to the far end of the trough and quickly drank while Rosalinda brushed her teeth. He followed her back to his crate and watched as she brushed the tangles out of her shoulder-length hair, tying it back with a faded red ribbon. She rinsed and refilled the bucket and brought it to the house.

"I'll see you later boy. Go back into your house. It's still cold." She scratched his head and neck and he crawled back into the crate.

She lit the oil lamp and quietly went about starting a fire in the stove and then put a pot of water on to warm. She did not know their routine, but warm water might be used for washing the lady's face, or cooking, or cleaning.

She put her toiletries back into her bundle and pulled out a leather-bound book, then sat at the table to read while she waited.

Twenty minutes passed before she heard someone stirring in the bedroom. A few minutes later Earl emerged fully dressed except for the last strap of his striped railroad bibs. He was in a rush and only nodded "Mornin," on his way out.

With one occupant up, she prepared dough for biscuits and set them in the oven to bake. After fifteen minutes Rosalinda began to wonder why Earl had not returned to the house. She slightly cracked open the door to peer out.

Earl had saddled one of the horses and was leading it back to the house. She quickly shut the door and repositioned herself at the table.

Earl came in and shut the door. "Got any food I can take along with me?" he asked.

"How many meals do you need?"

"I just need something for now and noontime I guess."

"All right, I can fix you up a package. Give me five minutes." She checked on the biscuits and seeing they were done, pulled them out placing them on the warming shelf.

Earl coughed and then said, "I may not be back for a week or so. There was a poster at the store sayin' they needed experienced railroad men right away to help with the Rock Island Railroad. They are building an extension that'll be goin' right through town. The pay is triple what I can scratch out of this place." His voice sounded nearly apologetic. "Anyways, I'll put up some money in advance at the store if you think Hattie needs anything." He reached into his pocket pulling out a few dollars in coin. "I gotta ask you to stay for at least a month. If they want me to go today, I won't be able to make it back to let Hattie know."

For once, Rosalinda had a strategic advantage in her life. Her stepfather was not there to negotiate her services for his own benefit. She contemplated what Earl told her while placing several biscuits and a few other items into a rectangular tin. She placed it in front of him and sat down.

"I would like an extra ten cents a day. This would be paid directly to me with the understanding that my stepfather is never to find out." There was no doubting the seriousness in her voice and eyes.

Earl pushed his chair back slightly. "I can arrange for you to get your extra pay through Mr. Hatcher at the store when you go to town."

"I'd like something else, too."

"Don't tell me you got another goddamned dog you want to bring over?"

Rosalinda laughed and for the first time she heard Earl laugh back. She looked directly at him and smiled. Her warmth helped relax him a bit and he sat back in his chair.

"No, nothing so drastic. I want to plant a vegetable garden twice the size you got laid out in the back. I'd like to sell most of the crop and give you thirty percent of the profit. It would be a little like I was share cropping."

"But that takes longer than a month," Earl explained.

"I know," she paused. "But you don't really know when your wife will be able to care for herself. The worse that could happen is you'll have a garden already started when you get back."

Earl thought for a moment. "Okay, but don't do so much that Hattie doesn't get the care I'm payin' you for." He got up and went into the bedroom. He returned in a few seconds with a half-filled duffel bag. Without saying anything more, he picked up the tin of food and walked towards the door.

He stopped as if he forgot something. "Tell Hattie I'll be back as soon as I can get us some decent money banked. Tell her I'll get a message to her as soon as I know where they are sending me." It was painfully obvious that Earl had not discussed

any of this with his wife. "You take care of her ya hear?" Without waiting for an answer, he walked out.

Rosalinda watched him through the window until the muffled sounds of the horses' hooves were drowned out by the sound of the water coming to a boil on the stove. She grabbed a flour-sack dish-towel and moved the pot to the cooler section of the stove top.

Shakespeare was scratching at the door and she walked out to join him. Last night's coolness captured more moisture than usual, and she smelled the hint of damp dirt as she reached down to pat her companion.

"Here you go," as she handed him a biscuit. "You know that you usually only eat supper, but we've got a lot to do today." He didn't eat it right away and took it into his little house instead. He set it down then positioned himself behind it. A few seconds later he started taking small bites until it disappeared.

The eastern sky began to brighten making vague shapes of the surroundings come into focus. She looked down the path and there was no sign that Earl had ever passed that way.

Returning to the kitchen a few moments later, she prepared enough corn meal mush for herself and Mrs. Curtis. Although this time she decided to eat first – knowing she may be too busy to eat after Mrs. Curtis awoke. When she finished her meal and cleaned her bowl, Rosalinda removed a small tin of black tea from her belongings. She carefully pinched out a measure of tea

into a cup of hot water. She did not have a tea strainer, so patiently waited for the leaves to steep and settle to the bottom.

As she sipped the tea she wondered if she should wake Mrs. Curtis now, or to go ahead and start her day. She listened closely for sounds from the bedroom and only heard the slow, steady breathing of a sleeping woman. Her cup now drained, Rosalinda decided it would be best to just make enough noise to waken her but not so obvious as to irritate the woman. She put more wood in the stove, moved the chairs, and lightly shuffled a few tin plates.

"Earl, Earl, what are you doing out there?" Hattie said in a sleepy voice. "I'll fix you something in a minute." The bed creaked as she shifted her weight to the edge of the bed.

Hearing this, Rosalinda went to the bedroom door but stood a few feet away. "Mrs. Curtis it's me. Rosalinda. May I come in?"

Hattie was confused. She only vaguely remembered a woman in the house last night but assumed she had been dreaming. She struggled for a moment trying to remember anything from yesterday, but nothing came into focus.

"Just a moment please." She slipped back down under the covers. "You can come in now."

Rosalinda stepped forward. "Good morning." Her voice was calm, assuring, and resonant. "I made you some breakfast. Would you like me to bring it in here, or would you like to try and sit at the table?"

A little more awake now, Hattie's memory slowly began to clear. This was the woman who showed her how to dip tortillas into soup, that delicious soup.

"Well, quite honestly, first I'd like to see if I can make it to the outhouse," she said looking passed Rosalinda. "Where's Earl?"

"He had to go into town. I'll tell you what I know after I've got you fed and freshened up."

Rosalinda looked about the floor and found a pair of woman-sized boots. "I guess these are yours. Slip your feet out of bed and I'll help you."

Hattie slipped her legs out from the covers letting her feet hang down to the floor. She then steadied herself placing her palms flat on the bed. Rosalinda moved the covers to the side and then knelt to slip one foot and then the other into the boots.

"Let me get you something for your shoulders." Rosalinda found a flannel shirt hanging from one of the clothing hooks and held it open. "It's still a little crisp out there."

Hattie looked up at her with a small thankful smile and slipped her arms into the shirt. She stood up slowly, unsure of how much strength she had. Her left hand reached for Rosalinda's waiting hand and then Rosalinda reached around Hattie's waist for better support.

"Ready?" Rosalinda asked.

"Ready."

They made their way to the front of the house carefully maneuvering through the bedroom door. From the front door it was just a short walk to the outhouse. Rosalinda, mindful of the need for privacy said, "just give me a good holler when you're ready. I'll be right over there."

Once Hattie was done Rosalinda helped her walk back.

When they reached the house, Shakespeare was waiting beside the door.

"Oh, who's this?"

"His name is Shakespeare. I've had him since he was a puppy."

"Can I touch him? Hattie asked.

"By the looks of his tail, I'd say he'd be pretty disappointed if you didn't."

Still hanging on to Rosalinda for support, Hattie leaned down to pat his head and then gave him a little rub under his chin. "So, have you written any good sonnets lately?"

Rosalinda answered, "no, I'm afraid he's hit a dry spell."

Hattie looked into the dog's soft brown eyes, "too bad Mr. Shakespeare, but don't let your hopes get down." She gave him one more pat then gingerly moved towards the door.

Once inside they made their way back to the bedroom and she helped Hattie sit down on the bed. "If I brought you a basin of warm water and a washcloth would you want to wash?"

"Yes, I think that would be fine."

Rosalinda went to the other room and returned with the basin, cloth, and a small towel. She moved the chair, so Hattie could easily reach it, and set the items on it.

"I'll go and fix your breakfast now," Rosalinda said as Hattie began to untie her night dress. Rosalinda noticed how light and smooth Hattie's skin looked where her bare skin was protected from the elements, then quickly turned her eyes away and left the room.

Rosalinda finished preparing Hattie's breakfast and was placing it on the table when Hattie came into the room. Despite her condition, she managed slip on a loose dress, but to her feet were bare. "I slipped off my shoes to put on my pants, but one of them went under the bed. I'm afraid I don't have enough energy to fetch it out."

"Tell you what, you sit down here and eat, and I'll get your shoes."

When Rosalinda returned she saw that Hattie hadn't started. "Is there something wrong?"

"No, Hattie sighed. "It's just been so long since I saw food like this. I just wanted to look at it for a few seconds."

The meal consisted of fresh cornmeal mush glistening with a large spoonful of honey, a biscuit with apricot preserves, and a sliced orange. By most accounts it was not a lavish spread. However, Earl's strict budget left them little more than a subsistence living. His plan was to buy a small herd of cattle and build on from there. Although there was now enough money set

aside for the herd, Earl said the hills needed the first flush of spring grasses, so they wouldn't need to buy feed the first year.

Rosalinda interjected, "Dr. Pierce prescribed a regimen of healthful food. You've got to eat nutritious meals for you and the baby."

She began to eat but held each mouthful a moment longer than normal, relishing the goodness.

After a few minutes she looked across the table, "have you eaten yet?"

"Yes, I ate earlier."

With two good meals and several extra hours of sleep, Hattie perked up and wanted to talk.

"Yesterday was such a blur. I don't remember much. I remember working out back, a little bit of the doctor visit, and that's about it. Oh, and I do remember the soup and tortillas. What's happened, and where's Earl?"

Rosalinda picked up the empty bowl while Hattie nibbled on the last of her biscuit.

"Your husband brought you to Dr. Pierce's house yesterday afternoon. Your condition is two-fold. You have an infection pretty common with expectant mothers called bacilluria. You're lucky you only have a mild case. This is what caused your discomfort when you urinated. To treat this, the doctor made you drink a solution of potassium citrate and sodium bicarbonate. That's what I gave you last night as well. When you're done here you'll be due for your second dose. The second part of your condition is just old-fashioned poor nutrition and exhaustion which is easy to treat, you've got to stick to eating right and resting when you're tired."

"So how did you get involved? You don't seem like the..." she hesitated, "like the other Mexican girls I've seen around town."

"Do you want the short or long version?"

"I've obviously got time, so I'll take the long version."

Rosalinda rarely talked about her personal life, and especially not to someone she just met. But her gentle voice and knowing she needed to tell this sick woman that her husband just took off, motivated her to open up more than usual.

Looking down at the table she began, "Well, my mother was born to a well-established family in Mexico." She paused and looked up at Hattie. She could see her immediate interest and continued. "She was well educated and could read and write fluent English. My father was from Connecticut and sold pharmaceuticals to physicians in Mexico City where his business dealings connected him to my mother's family."

"After they married, they lived in Mexico for a few years, but eventually my father's company moved him to West Texas where I was born. When I was ten, my father was beaten and left to die by a couple of drunken cowboys who wanted to teach him a lesson about mixing races. No one was ever charged, but then, the authorities didn't do much investigating. You did want the long version, right?"

Hattie nodded and listened intently. She was not particularly shocked by what Rosalinda said. She had heard of race problems though never from someone who was on the receiving end. Rosalinda continued telling her story in a matter-of-fact manner, neither soliciting nor attempting to arouse sympathy.

"Despite the loss of my father, my mother thought it was best to stay in America. Eventually my mother remarried, and we moved wherever and whenever my stepfather wanted to, and eventually landed here.

Through the years my mother and I helped Dr. Pierce with translating or nursing and so, well, here I am." She got up and brushed the crumbs off the table and into her hands. She then placed a large glass on the table and spooned in a measure of white powder from an amber-colored medicine bottle. As she poured water into the glass it foamed up nearly overflowing. "You should drink this while it's still has a fizz to it."

Hattie took a small sip, quickly placed the glass on the table, and made a very sour face.

"I found the best way to drink this is to deeply exhale, then drink it all at once. The less time you think about it the better."

Hattie looked like a child about to say, "Do I have to?" She took a deep breath, exhaled, and rhythmically swallowed until the glass was empty. "That was awful! How often do I have to drink that, that, vile sorcerer's potion?"

Rosalinda smiled, "Three times a day for five days."

For a few seconds Hattie licked the inside of her mouth like a dog with a bad tooth then asked, "you were saying that your mother wanted to stay in America?"

"How about we save the rest of my life story for later, if that's all right with you? I don't mind telling you, I just have quite a bit to do today. Besides, I need to tell you about Earl."

Oddly, Hattie had temporarily forgotten about Earl. It had been a long time since any conversation centered on something besides their homestead, the weather, and what comfort of life they would put off for the next year or two.

"Yes, where did Earl go? And, why?"

"Your husband said there was a poster in the store asking for help on the railroad for a new stretch. He said he would be gone for a week or so if they wanted him to start right away. He seemed very uncertain about the details, but said the pay was good. He also said he would put some advance money into the account at Hatcher's store in case he didn't get back right away."

Hattie was frowning.

"I told him that I'd stay on, but I'd want to plant a big vegetable patch to make a little cash. He said ok." Rosalinda saw that Hattie was still frowning.

"Men!" Hattie burst forth. "He didn't even discuss one word of this to me like I was a piece of furniture!" Hattie caught herself from ranting any further. "I'm sorry. It's just that it has been much harder than we imagined it would be."

Rosalinda replied, "I know. I think life is just harder than we all imagined it would be."

Hattie forced a weak smile which Rosalinda returned in kindness.

"You should probably rest now. Is there anything more I can do for you right now Mrs. Curtis?"

"Yes, please just call me Hattie. I feel old enough already."

"Okay, Hattie."

Hattie stood up on her own and shuffled slowly into the bedroom. Rosalinda heard the bed creak followed by a very large belch.

Chapter Seven – The Rabbit and the Cane

Earl was scratching out a note on the glass-covered counter as Mr. Hatcher finished gathering items for Earl's order.

Hattie,

I couldn't pass up the chance to earn four dollars a day. That's almost what we hoped to earn by the end of the next harvest – for only a week's worth of work! Hatcher said that Rosalinda can be trusted. She spent some time helping Dr. Pierce – heck that's better help then I could give you. The store account now has a surplus amount you can use. I will wire more when I get paid. The crew is leaving tomorrow, and we'll be out surveying for at least three weeks. Dr. Pierce said he'd stop by in a couple of days to check in on you. If you need me, ask for Bob Meeker at the land office. He'll know what area the crew is supposed to be working.

Earl

Holding the folded note out to Mr. Hatcher, Earl said, "I'd like to get this to my wife, but I don't know if you or Dr. Pierce will see the Mexican girl, uh Rosalinda, or my wife first. Would you mind checking with him tomorrow? I'd really appreciate it."

Mr. Hatcher nodded, "no problem. The Doc usually stops by every morning to pick up his mail and a small supply of lemon drops. He says he gives them out for coughs, but I've seen him pop a few as soon as he's outside. I think he has a sweet tooth."

Mr. Hatcher was ready to settle in for some conversation when Earl abruptly picked up his bundle. "Thanks for everything. See you in a few weeks."

Mr. Hatcher lifted his hand a few inches off the counter and partially waved as Earl walked out, "well adios to you."

Rosalinda found a piece of paper in the kindling box and smoothed it out. She then retrieved a pencil from her bag and went outside. She needed to make a full assessment of work in progress; animals, irrigation, feed, tools, and seed. It was not her ranch, her home, or her garden, but she would do her best for her employer and perhaps find the means to rid herself and her sister from Hector.

She opened the heavy barn doors and swung them wide open for maximum light.

Earl had taken the smaller of the two horses but had already fed and watered both of them. The stall needed mucking out and she scratched it down on the paper.

She noted several sacks of wheat seed lying up against the wall. She had heard people were successfully growing a winter variety and turning a profit. As she looked around the building she didn't see machinery for harvesting hay; perhaps he was planning on getting someone else to do it? She jotted down the number of bags and continued.

Rosalinda found a small basket hanging from a nail next to the bridle and carefully took it down. The light was too dim, so she brought it closer to the door. Inside were about a dozen brown envelopes with handwriting on the front of each. She lifted the first one; tomato, the second pole beans, hot peppers, summer squash, yellow squash, pumpkin, and watermelon. There was a treasure trove of seeds here. She would ask Hattie about them later as she set the basket down by the door.

She also noted that there were all the gardening tools she needed to get started.

Suddenly she was startled by the sound of something rooting around coming from outside the barn. She quickly walked around the side. Shakespeare froze, nose pointing straight, ears cocked forward. Rosalinda saw a ball of fur and blood struggling in a pile of discarded barbed wire. With each lunge, the small animal shred more of its fur and flesh.

Rosalinda could not stand to see an animal suffer. She understood that killing predators was sometimes required, and she also could hunt and kill for a meal. But this creature needn't suffer any longer than it already had.

She went back into the barn and found an axe and a bucket. The animal had calmed down substantially from the loss of blood allowing Rosalinda to move the barbed wire away enough execute a clean swing.

"God bless you rabbit and may San Francisco welcome your spirit." Her skillful swing sliced cleanly through the air and the rabbit was no longer suffering.

There was much to do but she decided to dress the animal now rather than risk it spoiling. With some reverence she placed the animal into the bucket and brought it to the shaded side of the barn. Shakespeare followed but minded himself not to disturb the contents of the pail when she set it down.

In the barn she found the few additional items she needed. First, she tied the hind legs together and hung it on a post to bleed. This would take several minutes, so she located a place to bury the guts. She returned and carefully pelted the animal without disturbing the meat. Next, she made a small slice into the hind legs between the bone and tendon, and then used a wooden stake to both spread the legs and to hang up the animal. She then nailed this stick to a post and placed the bucket under the carcass to let it bleed out again.

After finding a suitable spot, she dug a hole and returned to the hanging animal. She made one efficient cut into the belly just large enough to remove the entrails. She had been careful to not remove the fur from the animal's feet and now made four clean chops where the fur ended at each appendage. She wrapped these in a piece of burlap and set it aside.

She quickly buried the unusable animal parts and washed the fresh meat at the pump. While running the water over the flesh she thanked God for the gift. She then rinsed out the bucket and placed the liver and kidneys in it.

Rosalinda brought the rabbit into the kitchen, cut it into pieces and placed the meat into a pot of salt water and covered it, preventing it from spoiling for several hours. She then poured salt and water to cover the liver and kidneys in the bucket; Shakespeare would love fresh meat for dinner as well. As she was finishing her tasks, she heard Hattie getting up from her bed.

"I heard you rustling around out here. I cat-napped for a bit, but I hate just lying around," Hattie yawned.

"I know what you mean, but if you don't force yourself to rest, you'll be laid up even longer." Rosalinda glanced around the room, "do you have any books? Reading always helps to pass the time."

"I'm afraid I only have a Bible, a dictionary for who knows what reason, a couple of manuals on train brakes and boilers, and a book of poems by Elizabeth Barrett Browning. The latter I could almost recite. No, I'm afraid the library is pretty bare." She sounded sorry for herself again. Being forced to do nothing felt like punishment.

"Do you have writing paper?" Rosalinda asked.

"We've got some paper like a school tablet – not really stationery for formal letters or anything. Why?"

"We left in such a rush yesterday. I didn't have time to gather up everything I needed for a longer stay. I thought that if you wanted to write a letter or two today, I will make sure they get posted in town tomorrow on my way back."

"But won't that take a long time? I mean, is it okay for me to be left alone?"

"I won't be gone too long. When we had the wagon, we had to take the road or stay on mainly the flat stretches. I can get to my stepfather's house in twenty minutes on horseback. From there the town is just a fifteen-minute ride at an easy trot. If I follow the Pajarito Creek bed down through the south side of the draw at the Stiles' ranch I can get here from town in about thirty minutes." She used her finger to draw the imaginary route on the table while Hattie intently followed the course. They both looked up at the same time.

"That's quite amazing. Earl never mentioned a shortcut. He probably doesn't know about it," she added in a slightly cynical tone.

"Well, when you help a doctor out, people are always sharing their shortcuts. The Millingers used to live a mile down the road and one day Mr. Millinger smashed his arm up pretty bad trying to fix a wheel on a fully loaded wagon. His wife unhitched one of the horses and rode into town like a raiding Indian and the doctor followed her back using the shortcut. Later, when I had a chance to ride out here with him, he showed me the way. I know lots of shortcuts around here, but I keep most of them to myself."

Hattie nodded understandingly.

"So, do you think you may want to do some letter writing today?"

"Gosh, it's been months since my folks heard from us. My God, they don't even know I'm expecting!" Hattie declared.

"Good, then this 'rest time' will be time well spent," Rosalinda smiled, and Hattie then smiled in return.

Rosalinda continued surveying the ranch making notes as she went. At the long-shaded side of the barn, she stopped to examine a pile of discarded planks and stringers. Perhaps this was part of an old shed or a sheepherders' shack. She methodically sorted the lumber into types and sizes until it was laid out into usable piles. When she was done she walked back to the house stopping briefly at the pump to splash water on her face and neck.

Hattie managed to pull one of the chairs outside and was busily writing a letter to her parents. She looked up as Rosalinda approached.

"I decided not to tell my parents about being ill. It would just worry them for nothing," she said in an asking voice. "I'll just fill them in up to that point."

"I guess it wouldn't be lying to say you're going to be taking it a little easier. I think that might ease them some when they read you're expecting."

"Good idea," she put her pencil down and looked at the barn. "It sounded like you were doing some heavy work out there."

"I was sorting out that old pile of wood. Do you know if your husband has any plans for it?"

"Well, we were burning some of it in the stove a few months ago. Other than that, he had no plans."

"Would he mind if I used some of it?"

"No, I don't think so. He was saying it was going to be a good home for snakes and spiders. Go ahead, use what you want."

"Thanks," she replied. She opened the door and turned her head back. "If you want some help walking over to the outhouse, just call me or knock on the door. I've got to get supper started."

"I'm okay for now," she nodded and picked up her pencil to resume her letter.

In the kitchen, Rosalinda placed the rabbit meat in another pot and quickly browned it on all sides. Next, she reached into her pocket and brought out a tuft of wild sage. She carefully selected pieces suitable for cooking, then crushed and sprinkled it over the meat. She added enough water to simmer and covered it with a heavy lid. In a smaller pot she added Shakespeare's pieces, covered them with water and set it next to the larger pot to cook.

Rosalinda picked up the dirty pot and bucket and opened the door to wash them out at the pump. The sound of the door and the pot clanking in the bucket woke Hattie up from an unplanned nap.

"I'm sorry, I didn't know you were sleeping," Rosalinda apologized.

"I didn't know I was sleeping either," Hattie yawned.

Rosalinda walked to the pump and rinsed out the blood while Hattie watched, puzzled, from her chair. She propped the bucket and pot upside down on a flat rock to dry and walked back to the house.

"What was that blood from?" Hattie asked half-worried.

"We're going to have fresh rabbit for supper. That was just a little blood left from dressing it out."

Hattie was amazed. When did anyone have time to hunt? "I didn't hear a shot. How did we get a rabbit?"

Rosalinda thought it sounded funny that somehow "we" got a rabbit.

"I'm afraid he got himself trapped in some barbed wire. He injured himself struggling to get free," she paused and looked out across the fields. "I thought that putting him out of his misery would be a blessing for all of us." There was sadness and sympathy in her voice that Hattie unconsciously found engaging.

"Yes," Hattie said softly, "let's mention this when we say grace."

Shakespeare appeared from around the corner of the house and sat down next to Hattie. She automatically began to pet him and scratch around his ears. The dog, in obvious ecstasy, lowered his head on her lap.

"Don't get too comfortable boy," Hattie said. "I've got to make a pilgrimage over to that little house."

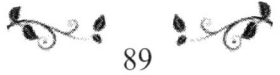

Rosalinda extended her hand for support. As they walked, Rosalinda asked, "How's your letter writing coming along?"

"Maybe I'll finish up right after supper. My folks sure will be pleased to hear from me."

"Sounds like a good plan. I think it would also be a good plan to lay down for a spell after you have finished your letter. I'll let you know when dinner is ready."

Rosalinda woke Hattie up about four o'clock for supper and on her own, she shuffled her way to the table and sat down.

The table was set with one bowl, a cup, spoon, and fork. Grabbing a dish towel, Rosalinda lifted the black Dutch oven and set it in the middle of the table. "Smell's wonderful," Hattie commented. "I'm afraid I've never been much of a cook."

Rosalinda lifted the lid, setting it upside down on the table.

"Dumplings?" Hattie asked. "I haven't had dumplings since, since we left Texas."

Rosalinda scooped out a healthy portion of dumplings, rabbit, wild onions, and gravy into Hattie's bowl.

"You eat what you can, especially the meat. The iron and protein in it will help you the most. Save the dumplings for last."

"Aren't you going to eat with me?"

"Thank you. I'd like that."

Rosalinda got herself a bowl and spoon, ladled out a portion, and sat down across from her. Hattie waited for Rosalinda to finish serving herself and then started to say grace.

"Heavenly Father, thank you for sending us this rabbit today. We are grateful for all your gifts and pray you will watch over Earl wherever he is. Amen."

The women ate heartily, both taking second helpings as large as the first. Neither talked during the first bowl, but Hattie slowed down her eating pace enough to start a conversation.

"When will you be leaving tomorrow?" Hattie asked.

Rosalinda put down her spoon and pointed to her mouth indicating she still had a mouthful to chew and swallow.

She sat back in the chair and thought for a second. "I'd like to get an early start. I'll wake you for breakfast a little earlier than today and take off after you've eaten and cleaned up. Is that all right? I should be back around noon."

"I'm a little embarrassed to say this, but, well, I'm not sure if I can make it to the outhouse and back without help." She said in a worried tone.

"I understand," Rosalinda said. "I saw an old basin full of nails in the barn. I thought that tonight I'd put together a little seat stand for it. Of course, it won't be as fancy as the commodes in the Albuquerque hotels, but it should be quite functional."

"Are you always like this?"

"Always like what?"

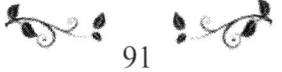

"Well, thinking way ahead like that, planning out what you're going to do and figuring how to do it? I can't imagine making a commode stand and, and you had already thought about it before I ever mentioned it."

Rosalinda took this as a compliment but felt a little embarrassed.

They both sat quietly for a few moments. Hattie thought that Earl didn't want to have a chamber pot in the house, so they didn't.

Rosalinda took a sip of water and said, "My mother was always making me figure things out. If we needed to go to several places, she'd have me figure the best route and explain why. If something had to be fixed or made, she'd have me figure out if we could do it ourselves before spending the money or being dependent on others."

"Your mother sounds like a woman of great strength and wisdom. I'd love to meet her." Hattie said with a smile.

Rosalinda turned her eyes away and looked saddened.

"I'm sorry. Did I say something wrong?"

"You're right," Rosalinda looked back to Hattie. "A woman of great strength and wisdom, but she's gone now. It's been three years."

"I'm so sorry. Do you mind me asking? Was it an illness?"

"No – she died from a lack of options."

Hattie found this statement to be totally confusing but decided not to pursue this area of conversation.

"Did the dog eat yet?" Hattie asked.

"Oh, I'll throw together a dish with our scraps and will add some rabbit parts I cooked up for him on the side."

The change of topic was enough to lighten the room once again.

"He's a nice dog, but why do you call him Shakespeare? Are you an enthusiast of the literary arts?" Hattie teased.

Rosalinda finished her supper and got up to place her dish in the oval-shaped wash pan. "Actually, although I've been known to read a play or two, he was named after a town up north towards the Colorado border. His previous owner picked him up there when he was a puppy. He moved down here with Shakespeare and was going to train him to help him herd sheep." Rosalinda talked as she cleared the table. "He got Shakespeare pretty well trained, but one day the man stepped into a nest of scorpions."

"Oh God, how awful – scorpions!" Hattie shivered.

"Normally a man can survive a single sting, but this poor fellow sustained four. By the time he got to Dr. Pierce, he was almost dead. You know he really must have loved that dog. His last words were, 'Find a good home for Shakespeare.' Anyway, Doctor Pierce gave me the dog the next day."

"Well, he looks quite happy to be with you."

"He's my best friend – Mr. Hatcher is a close second."

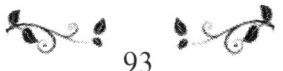

Hattie pushed her chair away from the table and slowly walked back to the bedroom. When she returned she brought back the partially-written letter and her writing materials. Placing them on the table, she sat back down.

By then, Rosalinda had the dog's meal ready. "I'm going to be working in the barn after I feed Shakespeare," she said holding a large tin plate full of food. "If you need me just bang on this fry pan with the stoker, and I'll be here quick."

"Thank you. I appreciate your thoughtfulness."

When the sun had almost set, Rosalinda returned from the barn to find Hattie stuffing the letter to her folks in an envelope.

"I'm afraid that I don't have any postage stamps here." She turned the envelope over and licked the flap. Besides, I wouldn't know how much to put on it."

Rosalinda sat down. "That's all right. Mr. Hatcher will take care of it and put it on your account." She could see that Hattie was looking at what Rosalinda had in her hand.

Rosalinda handed her a walking cane.

"Where did you get this?" She was quite astonished that Rosalinda found this anywhere on the property.

Rosalinda only shrugged and smiled.

Hattie examined it more closely. It had just been made. She recognized the handle; it was from the hoe whose trowel head broke off a couple of weeks ago. But it had been sanded smooth, rubbed with oil, and then polished to a shine. The "T" shaped grip was made from a concealed pipe connector that had been

carefully wrapped with rabbit hide and fastened with braided pieces of leather stripping.

"You did, uh, you made this didn't you?"

"Well just in case I don't make it back before nature calls…anyway, I thought this would give you a little more freedom." Rosalinda was pleased with her work but found no need to make much of it.

Hattie kept looking at her gift and thought, "How does one create something like this out of nothing? She could have just found me an old stick; that's what Earl would have done."

Hattie looked up and said, "Thank you very much. Do you think I could try it out now; is it ready?"

Rosalinda nodded yes. "I can shorten it some if it's too long."

Hattie, with her new cane, got up, walked around the room and returned to her seat. "No, I think that it will be just fine."

"Just remember that it's only for balance. If you feel really weak it won't help you very much. Which reminds me, did you drink your medicine?

"Yes, I did, and it tasted as vile as it did the first time. Are you sure that potion works?"

"I don't know. Maybe it's just a motivator to get well." She said with a wink. "When I go tomorrow do you want me to take Shakespeare, or would you like him to stay here with you?"

Hattie thought for a second, "If you don't mind, I'd like for him to stay here. I feel more justified talking to a dog than talking to myself."

"Well, be careful what you say. I swear he understands everything I tell him."

A few moments of silence passed between them with only the sound of the night breeze catching the door jamb. Rosalinda got up, fetched a few pieces of wood from the box then placed them in the stove and said, "I think it's going to get a little colder tonight."

Hattie, who was still studying her cane, looked up. "Do you think the dog will be warm enough out there?"

"He does fine as long as he can keep dry. He still has most of his winter coat and he's used to being outside most of the time. Thanks for asking. Most people never think about how animals feel until the poor thing is on his deathbed. Then, if they're lucky, they'll just shoot the poor thing, and blame it for getting sick or hurt in the first place."

"Oh, I made a little commode for you. It's just outside."

Rosalinda went out and brought back what looked like a wooden crate with an oval-shaped hole cut into its side. She placed it in the corner of the bedroom then went to retrieve the basin and a board. When she came back she positioned the crate with the hole facing up and then slipped the board onto runners creating a shelf several inches below the top to hold the basin. She came back into the main room and sat across from Hattie.

"I think you're all set in there. You won't have to use the outhouse if you don't feel you can make it, or don't want to go outside. It's not pretty but it's functional."

"Thank you. I'm sure it will do just fine."

It was getting late but neither wanted to be the first to call it a night. They talked for a while longer until finally Rosalinda said, "Do you need anything before I turn in? I'll be leaving early."

"Oh, I guess it is getting late. I think I can manage to get into my nightgown tonight. Using her cane, she made her way to the bedroom. "Goodnight Rosalinda. Thank you for the cane and everything."

"Goodnight Hattie. You're welcome."

Hattie lifted her gown off its hook, slipped it over her head, then sat down on the bed. As she looked at the box-commode in the corner she noticed even this most unglamorous of objects, a commode, was given the care in its making. Every surface that could possibly touch her skin was sanded smooth and Rosalinda even thought to bring in a pile of wiping papers from the outhouse.

She enjoyed the sense of being cared for; it wasn't that Earl didn't care for her like any hardworking husband might, but this was care with thought and sensitivity. She slipped her feet under the covers and as she reached to extinguish the lamp, she lightly touched the fur on the handle of the cane.

After a moment she rolled over and faced the window. How strange, she thought, this was the first time she and Earl had been separated. One would expect many new brides left alone, especially in the company of a stranger, would be distraught and weeping over being abandoned. Instead, she contentedly looked at the few bright stars framed in the window and drifted pleasantly to sleep.

Chapter Eight – The Ghost

The morning was still chilly as Rosalinda rounded the final bend to her stepfather's house. As she got closer, her heightened stress quickened the puffs of fog-like vapor from her nose. This confirmed her belief; she hated the place. Even the horse seemed reluctant to go further and nearly came to a stop.

"Your instincts are right, compadre," as she patted him on the neck, "but we won't be long." She cautiously rode by the rooster pen and then to the back of the house before dismounting. There was no sign of Hector or his brother. "This is good," she thought. "Cecelia, she called, as she stepped in the house. Cecelia, she called again. But again, no answer.

A little puzzled, Rosalinda walked back to the rooster pen. She was surprised to see that all of Hector's fighting cocks were gone. Usually, he took his two healthiest cocks to fight, saving the others to recuperate for the next competition. Although Hector boasted to every male within thirty miles that Cecelia was never home alone, he would have left her behind to care for the remaining roosters. This was even more puzzling but decided not to waste time dwelling on it.

Walking to the back of the house, she whistled loudly. From a clump of distant bushes, a burro brayed excitedly. "Hey there boy, come on." She clapped her hands and he trotted towards her.

"Did anyone feed you?" she asked. Assuming he had not been fed, she walked to the lean-to and retrieved a quarter square of alfalfa, splitting it between the horse and the burro.

Rosalinda returned to the house and packed a large carpet bag of clothes and personal items. Suddenly she remembered the "secret can" that she and Cecelia shared. There were a precious few dollars, primarily earned by Rosalinda, for Cecelia if she could ever find the right time to run away.

She hurried to the cupboard, stood on a chair, and reached to grab the hidden can of dry mustard. She shook it, but the familiar rattle of coins was absent. She pried off the lid to find only a folded note. Perhaps by habit, Rosalinda removed the paper, but carefully replaced the lid and returned the can to its designated spot.

She stepped down and read the note, written in Spanish.

Rosalinda

My only friend. Papa will be gone for two weeks to fight his cocks in San Jon, then to Logan. This is my chance. I sold papa's other cocks for $100. I am going to Pueblo, Colorado. Father Palo says he knows a young priest who may help me find work. When I can, I will send word to Dr. Pierce or Father Palo.

Via Con Dios,

Cecelia

Rosalinda refolded the note and did not know if she should cry with happiness or loss. They had been planning Cecelia's escape for over a year, but it was a shock that she actually went through with it. She wiped away her tears and after a few deep breaths was ready to focus on her original mission.

Armed with the knowledge that Hector would be away, she could plan another trip should circumstances allow.

Within an hour she had loaded several burlap sacks on the horse. On the burro, she arranged two wooden crates, each containing three chickens, feed, and several jars of vegetables and fruit she had canned from the previous year. She was careful to leave enough of everything behind so Hector would not notice anything missing.

For now, God would have to tend her garden. With some luck, the late spring rains would sustain it without her daily care. Her goats were nibbling on some brush and a kid goat tagging along with its mother; they would be fine for now as well.

Once the burro and the horse lifted their heads from the wooden water trough, she connected the burro's lead to her saddle.

"Time to go, boys' she announced and led them over the hill towards town.

She didn't want to draw attention to herself, so she bypassed the Mexican side of town. She took a curve to the south and finally ended up at the back door of Dr. Pierce's house.

He saw her approach from his kitchen window and walked outside to greet her.

"Rosalinda," he said warmly, "Come in and have a glass of lemonade with me." He took the horse's reins and tied them to the back-porch railing.

"Why that's the best invitation I've had – well, since the last time we had lemonade. I'd love a glass." She slid off the horse and brushed off her clothes."

"Well, you'll like this lemonade even better. The train started bringing in ice on a regular basis."

She sat down at his kitchen table while he filled her glass and then topped off his.

"You noticed, of course, that Cecelia wasn't at home?" he asked.

"Yes, and I found her note."

"Good, good," he said in a serious tone. "Timing couldn't have been better," he continued. "The night you left, Hector nearly raped her. But he was too drunk to chase her once she got out of the house. He finally took his bottle into the cock shed and just passed out. Apparently, he only had his fighting cocks on his mind when he woke up and took off for San Jon for some big fighting match. As soon as he left, Cecelia grabbed the other cocks."

Dr. Pierce reassuringly placed his hand on hers. "As soon as anyone hears anything we'll get word to you. You know your sister is no dummy. As soon as she got to town, she went down to the railroad siding. She found a couple Mexicans more than willing to buy those cocks, and they were on their way to Odessa! Hah!"

Dr. Pierce drank the rest of his lemonade and set the glass down. "I see you're taking some of your chickens for a ride. Don't they have any of their own up there?"

"No, they don't and have little of anything else. No wonder she got so run down. Anyway, Mr. Curtis will be gone for several weeks, maybe longer, to do some railroad work. My chickens are laying more eggs than Hector can eat – not that he'd know how to cook them with Cecelia gone.

Rosalinda swallowed the last of her drink and looked at the ice. "You're right; this is the best lemonade I ever had." She paused as if she was studying the crystal shards, "If all goes well at the Curtis place, I might be able to save up a little and eventually join Cecelia."

Dr. Pierce pulled on his earlobe, "Well, they don't strike me as being able to raise your wages much."

"I know, but Mr. Curtis already gave me a raise, and gave me permission to put in a vegetable garden and I can sell the produce. At the rate this town is growing, I shouldn't have any trouble making a few dollars."

"Well, it sounds like a good plan if Hector doesn't ruin it. Anyway, you know that I'll give you a holler if I can use you around my office. Like you said the town is growing so I suspect my business will grow as well."

About a mile out of town, Rosalinda slid off the horse and walked back to check the burro's load. The chicken crates made the poor thing appear almost as tall as the horse. "You're a good boy. I'm sorry the chickens made a mess on your back. We'll take care of that when we get to Hattie's place."

She cinched up a couple of ropes then climbed back on the horse. She glanced back over her shoulder to see if, by some miracle, Cecelia might appear. But, of course, she knew that she would not. It was not her nature to dwell on things out of her control, but this was hard. She gave the horse a gentle kick.

The situation with her sister frustrated but did not shock her. As Cecelia matured, Hector became more and more obsessed with watching the girl.

As she rode on, she recalled that late last spring, while picking string beans from her garden, she saw Hector looking into the window of their house. At first, she thought he was just talking to her sister. But then it appeared from her own squatted position that he was going to urinate on the side of the house. Puzzled as to why he would do this, she straightened up to watch. He then began to slightly thrust his pelvis forward with both hands remaining low in front of him. She could only see his back

as his movements, now becoming rhythmic, became faster. His elbows began to move quickly back and forth like pistons on a locomotive when he suddenly turned. She immediately squatted back down behind the bean poles, hidden from his view. She could see now that he was holding his erect penis and was sliding his grip up and down its shaft. She heard him groan "Aye, aye, aye!" as the white mucous-like fluid spurted on to the ground. She turned away shaking from disgust. Her sister was no longer safe. Before she could regain her breath, Hector buttoned his fly and was now happily yelling profanities at the chickens.

She waited behind the bean poles until he disappeared into the rooster shed. Quietly, she quickly went into the house and carefully shut the door behind her. She walked back to their bedroom to find her sister taking a nap, totally unaware that she had just been violated by her father. Rosalinda, sitting on the edge of the bed, wondering what to tell her.

Cecelia turned and opened her eyes, still quite groggy she asked. "Is it time for me to start dinner?"

"No, no you can rest a little while longer," as she gave her sister an affectionate pat on her ankle. About a mile out of town, Rosalinda slid off the horse and walked back to check the burro's load. The chicken crates made the poor thing appear almost as tall as the horse. "You're a good boy. I'm sorry the chickens made a mess on your back. We'll take care of that when we get to Hattie's place."

She cinched up a couple of ropes then climbed back on the horse. She glanced back over her shoulder to see if, by some

miracle, Cecelia might appear. But, of course she knew that she would not. It was not her nature to dwell on things out of her control, but this was hard. She gave the horse a gentle kick.

The situation with her sister frustrated but did not shock her. As Cecelia matured, Hector became more and more obsessed with watching the girl.

As she rode on, she recalled that late last spring, while picking string beans from her garden, she saw Hector looking into the window of their house. At first, she thought he was just talking to her sister. But then it appeared from her own squatted position that he was going to urinate on the side of the house. Puzzled as to why he would do this, she straightened up to watch. He then began to slightly thrust his pelvis forward with both hands remaining low in front of him. She could only see his back as his movements, now becoming rhythmic, became faster. His elbows began to move quickly back and forth like pistons on a locomotive when he suddenly turned. She immediately squatted back down behind the bean poles, hidden from his view. She could see now that he was holding his erect penis and was sliding his grip up and down its shaft. She heard him groan "Aye, aye, aye!" as the white mucous-like fluid spurted on to the ground. She turned away shaking from disgust. Her sister was no longer safe. Before she could regain her breath, Hector buttoned his fly and was now happily yelling profanities at the chickens.

She waited behind the bean poles until he disappeared into the rooster shed. Quietly, she quickly went into the house and

carefully shut the door behind her. She walked back to their bedroom to find her sister taking a nap, totally unaware that she had just been violated by her father. Rosalinda, sitting on the edge of the bed, wondering what to tell her.

Cecelia turned and opened her eyes, still quite groggy she asked. "Is it time for me to start dinner?"

"No, no you can rest a little while longer," as she gave her sister an affectionate pat on her ankle. "We've got to plan this, Cecelia," Rosalinda said. "or it won't work. We may only have one chance, and we need to be ready."

Cecelia nodded in agreement.

"First we must get some money and hide it. I have twelve dollars sewn into my serape. Let's put ten away in…" She searched the room, but nothing seemed satisfactory. She walked into the kitchen, her eyes still searching. Finally, she pulled a stool over to see the cans on the top pantry shelf. "Perfect," she said, climbing off the stood.

Cecelia quickly walked in. "What did you find?"

"A can of dry mustard. Remember when I made you a mustard plaster last winter?" Rosalinda asked.

"Santa Maria, I will never forget," Cecelia said as she watched her sister pour the contents onto a piece of paper.

"Here," Rosalinda said, handing her the folded paper containing the yellow-brown powder. "Throw this with the wind but be careful not to get it into your eyes!"

Cecelia nodded and took the package outside. Meanwhile, Rosalinda gathered up her serape and a knife and sat on the edge of her bed. Cecelia returned, and Rosalinda glanced up to make sure it was not Hector, and then returned to removing a few key stitches. Pulling one bill out at a time, she handed them to Cecelia who carefully rolled them into each other. Finally, when there were ten bills, they placed them in the can and tapped the lid back into place. Cecelia put the can on the top shelf, out of sight and hidden by a few more cans and rarely used items.

Rosalinda spoke, "I will do whatever I can to earn some money, but it's almost impossible when Hector is home. I guess what I'm trying to say is that I can't be here to protect you and at the same time, earn money so you can run away. Tomorrow I will make an excuse to go into town. I think I can sell my dried beans and chilies to Mr. Hatcher a little earlier this year.

"What will you tell Hector?" Cecelia questioned.

"I will tell him that I will ask Dr. Pierce for some medicine for him," Rosalinda responded in low, cool words.

"Medicine? He's not sick." Cecelia shook her head in confusion.

"Not now, but he will be after breakfast." Rosalinda gave a slight grin.

"Rosalinda," Cecelia wondered, "where is Papa now?"

"He's in the shed. The last time I saw him he was knocked out. The wind jarred loose a bucket he had hung up, and it hit him on the head. But he was so drunk I think he would have passed

out anyway." Rosalinda decided not to tell her about the pitchfork or pouring most of the remaining liquor over his body.

Hector woke up lying on the floor of the shed. His head felt like it had been cracked open. He gingerly rolled over and touched the back of his head with his hand. It was tender and wet with blood, and his memory was totally blurred. The bottle was back on the crate with barely a swallow left. The ax was back in its place. The only thing out of place was the large galvanized bucket which usually hung from the rafter and was now on the floor. Still wobbly, Hector slowly opened the door. The earlier raging wind was now only a breeze and the chickens were leisurely pecking at little pieces of grit and rock. The pitchfork leaned against the cottonwood tree just as it had this morning. He walked out into the air, leaned against the wall of the shed, and held a hand over his bucket-shaped wound. "That's fucking bad tequila," he said.

The front door banged open as Hector spilled into the house. For a second, he just stood there to find his bearings and then stumbled to his bedroom. Waiting on the dresser was a half-emptied bottle of tequila he knew was good. He took a long drink and lay down on the bed. Staring at the ceiling, he was pretty sure the ghost was real.

Rosalinda waited until she heard Hector's familiar snore before entering his room. She quickly found the open bottle of tequila; there was always a bottle in his room. She snatched it up from the window sill and brought it to the kitchen.

"Here, you hold the funnel," Rosalinda said.

Cecelia placed the tin funnel into the neck of the bottle, holding it steady.

Rosalinda carefully poured several ounces of white kerosene into the tequila.

"Don't you think this might kill him?" Cecelia asked.

"I suppose it would if he drinks enough of it, but it should burn too much on the way down before he ingests enough. If he dies, I don't think the authorities will blame us. I heard that some cowboys in Las Cruces died from some bad liquor a month ago. They'll just assume he got some of the same stuff."

"Well, maybe we should just add more kerosene and be done with him," Cecelia urged.

"As I said, he would probably stop drinking it before he gets enough to kill him." Rosalinda stopped pouring and set the can down on the floor.

"I just need to get into town to make arrangements, okay?"

Cecelia nodded.

Rosalinda quietly returned the bottle to the window sill as Hector continued to snore in a slow rhythmic pattern.

Then softly Rosalinda whispered, "I hope you wake up thirsty."

Hector slept but not peacefully. His wife was in his dreams and she was talking back. The disobedient bitch! The man ruled

the family, the man made the decisions, and the man owned everything. How dare she say I spent her money? The cunt, who does she think she is?

He tossed in his bed, reliving those final moments as he struck his wife in anger and fury. He saw himself stomping out of the house. She was supposed to stay put but no, she had to get up and follow him to the shed.

"It's my money, you bastard!"

With his back turned it felt as if her words were talons and were digging into his flesh. There was no thought, no need for thought when you're right. The ax handle came down hard against her temple and she crumpled down to the dirt floor like a wet sheet.

Her collapse disappointed him; one swing was barely what she had coming to her. But there is no satisfaction gained from hitting a lifeless body. He wiped his brow and spat on the floor. He watched her for several seconds before he knelt for a closer look. He cautiously leaned over and watched as a fly landed on her face. She did not twitch, and he smirked in morbid satisfaction.

Suddenly, her eyes opened, and her gaze pierced his eyes like a butcher knife. She took a heroic breath and said, "I'll get you. Even after death, I swear I'll get you." A moment later, she was dead.

He gasped himself awake and saw the familiar cracked ceiling and the window sill. He blinked twice to get his bearings.

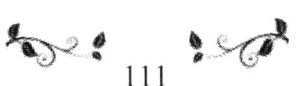

In relief, he rolled over and thought "It's only a dream; she's dead and can't talk."

Chapter Nine – I Can Do This

There were six men on the railroad survey team. Although Earl did not have any of the surveying skills, he was more than glad to be a general hand. After breakfast the men normally broke up into pairs leaving Earl behind. He did the cleanup and got things ready to move to the next designated camp. From time to time, he helped the surveyors move their equipment, especially when the terrain was too rough to navigate without at least one free hand.

Earl didn't care much for the chuck-wagon tasks he was assigned, but anything was better than the hard, monotonous ranch life he escaped. Everything about the homestead was harder than he had imagined, and he began to resent the demands, both real and in his restless dreams. He hated the long days, missed working with other men, to joke with, and to challenge. He figured that he and Hattie had talked about all there was of any interest. Now the only thing left was to talk about the work that needed to be done.

He especially missed the railroad; the whole future of the country depended on it. If a man worked the railroad, he was respected, and he had bragging rights. He knew that taking this job gave him a foot in the door with the company. So, for now,

any job would do. Besides, it felt great to have real conversations with real men.

A few weeks into the job a man on horseback rode into camp with two pack mules loaded with provisions. Earl vaguely remembered him from the railroad office.

"What's all this for?" Earl inquired.

The man slipped off his horse, took off his hat, wiped the inside band with a handkerchief and then wiped the beads of sweat from his much-receded hairline.

"When will the men be back?"

"Should be anytime now if their stomachs tell them it's time for supper," Earl said with a little irritation.

"Well," he said placing his hands on his lower back and stretching, "best we wait for the others." He groaned, and Earl heard a few vertebrae pop for his efforts. The man put his hat back on and started walking towards the mules, but then turned back to Earl. "My name's Nathan Horstetter but the boys call me Horse for short."

Earl approached and extended a hand. "My name's Earl Curtis."

"You wouldn't be one of them Earl's I heard about back in Texas that got mixed up with some other guy named Earl trying to unload a shipment of pipe are yeh?"

"'Fraid so," Earl answered with an embarrassed laugh.

"Well," smiled Horse, "the story got around. No shame on you, in fact, it made you kinda out to be a hero of sorts, you know, making that citified Earl look like he couldn't find his pecker with two hands."

Earl suddenly really liked this man. "You want a hand unloading the mules?"

"Sure. You take that one there." Horse gestured over to the animal to his right.

When they finished, the survey team started filing in. They all knew Horse and greeted him with slaps and fake punches. They were puzzled, however, by this unscheduled visit.

"I got some good news and some bad news boys and let's be clear; I'm just the messenger."

The men stepped in closer to hear what he had to say.

"The good news is that you'll all be getting a bonus when you get back. But, the bad news is that you'll have to work straight through to the west marker point before you can head back. Sorry boys, but you won't be able to take that break between sections." The track would be laid through Roy and French and finally end at the coal fields in Dawson, the end spot marked on the survey map. This meant at least an additional two months. It was possible that the surveyors would need more time in the field to merge with the construction crews to support the actual grading processes.

"How much is the bonus?" The eldest surveyor asked.

"One month of your current wage, whatever that might be." Then Horse added, "If ya don't want it, you'll have to quit now, and you'll be paid up to today. But, if you sign these forms, the office will set up a draw account for your wives. You can note how much in case you don't want them writing off to Sears and Roebuck without your permission." When he pulled out a small stack of folded sheets from his back pocket, the men all nodded and grabbed a form.

Earl knew what he wanted to do but asked, "Would you mind taking a letter back to the wife?" A few other men nodded that they needed to do the same.

"No problem, but it's you that'll need to do the explaining. I'm just going to deliver them to Hatcher's store. I'll be headin' back first thing in the morning.

> *Hattie*
>
> *It looks like we won't have a break for at least eight weeks. The best part is that they will give us a big bonus for staying on. I've set up a draw account for you at the office to take care of your basics and to pay for the girl on a regular basis. She might ask for the money in advance, but there won't be enough in your draw account to do that. Besides, those people would just take the money and run, leaving you high and dry.*
>
> *I'm sure that I can settle up with the doc when I get back.*
>
> *Earl*

Rosalinda last talked with Dr. Pierce a week ago. She had been waiting on his back porch for thirty minutes while he finished pulling a bad molar out of Riley Babcock's mouth. She was anxious for news of her sister and of her stepfather's reaction to her disappearance. Unconsciously, she picked the eyes out of every potato from the small pile someone had left him for payment.

Finally, she heard someone leaving by the front door with an apparent attempt to say, "Thank you doc," through a mouthful of gauze. A few seconds later, Dr. Pierce stepped out onto the back porch.

He glanced down at the potatoes and then to Rosalinda, "There, you've done it."

"Done what?" Rosalinda asked.

"Blinded a perfectly healthy group of *Solanum Tuberosums*."

"What? Oh, sorry." Rosalinda mustered a polite smile acknowledging the doctor's attempt to put her at ease. She stood up nervously rubbing her hands together.

"Do you have any news of my sister? Did my stepfather set out to find her?"

He unfolded a handkerchief to clean his glasses. "I haven't heard anything about your sister, probably too early yet for news to get here. I did hear an interesting rumor about your stepfather though. Mind you it's just rumor, so you'll have to stop by the deputy's office to get better information."

Rosalinda cocked her head like a dog listening to a strange sound. "What's the rumor?" Her mind raced back to the bottle of tainted tequila. Perhaps he finally drank it? Rosalinda remembered that when he awoke that afternoon, he merely stuffed the bottle down into his pants pocket. It could have been sitting around for months; maybe it fell behind something in the shed?

He scratched at a patch of stubble on his face, "It seems there was quite the brawl in San Jon."

"That's not unusual," Rosalinda satirically remarked.

"Well, the rumor is that Hector slipped some tequila into the drinking water of one of his competitor's birds right before the last fight. The strange thing is, the bird barely got a scratch on it when it just keeled over and died. At any rate, Hector grabbed up his winnings and was long gone before the owner of the other cock got a good whiff of the water."

Dr. Pierce continued, "But apparently they eventually caught up with him near Logan and cut him up pretty bad."

"Is he dead?"

"I don't know. Maybe the deputy can answer that. I never wish for anyone to die, but I sure won't feel a bit sorry if he didn't make it."

"I'll go over there right now. Thanks, doctor."

The deputy was emptying the basket of coffee grinds on an old newspaper when Rosalinda stepped in. "Be with you in just a tad. This will turn into a mess if I let it sit."

"How are you, Rosalinda? I had a feeling you'd be stopping by soon." Deputy Silas Specture was a thin, middle-aged man who moved from Wisconsin after reading countless nickel novelettes about cowboys and Indians. At eighteen he had hoped to participate in taming the West. But save for the routine drunkenness, routine gunfights, routine arguments of fence lines and pasture rights, there was very little taming left to do. The real outlaws: Billy the Kid, Sam Bass, Jesse James, and the Younger brothers, were all gone or locked up by the time he put on his star. So now he had a plump wife, three children, and was surprisingly quite content.

"I'm doing well Silas. Dr. Pierce told me what he heard about Hector but said what he knew was rumor. Can you tell me something official?"

"Well, I don't know if he poisoned the other fella's rooster or not, but there was a pretty bad knife fight in Logan involving Hector. I got a wire yesterday afternoon from the Logan office. It indicated that both Hector and the man who came after him died from their wounds a couple hours after the altercation. Here's the wire if you'd like to read it over."

Rosalinda sat down and read the telegram twice and began to cry. Silas reached into his back pocket and produced a freshly laundered handkerchief. She sobbed into it with a flood of pent-up tears.

Silas was confused. He put his hand on her shoulder then softly said, "I didn't know you cared for the man. I'm sorry for your loss."

"No, no you don't understand. What I couldn't do, somehow God did for me." She blew her nose, took a deep breath, and patted his hand. She smiled then said, "What do you need me to do?"

"Not much. You won't have to identify him. Hector had already seen the inside of their jail more than once, so the sheriff signed the certificate. You can arrange to bring him back," Rosalinda was already shaking her head no, "Or, I can wire back to them stipulating to give him the services normally rendered an incarcerated person."

"Yes, that would be fine. Could I impose on you to request a copy of the death certificate?"

"No imposition whatsoever. Glad to oblige."

After leaving the deputy's office, Rosalinda picked up a few needed items from the store.

"Excuse my language, but God's good earth is better off with that S.O.B. dead," Mr. Hatcher exclaimed as he scooped out candy and folded the portion into the brown wrap. "This is on

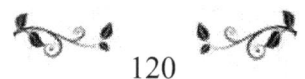

me. As well as the thirty-seven dollars and fifteen cents Hector owed me. I'm not going to pass his debt along to you."

"No, you don't have to do this. I, I can."

Mr. Hatcher put up his hands motioning her to stop.

"Look, your mother did a whole lot more good in this world than she ever got back in return. And you? You've grown up to be so much like her." He paused, took a breath and exhaled. "This is my gift to your mother. Please let me do this for her."

Rosalinda saw a hint of tears in his eyes. Perhaps Mr. Hatcher cared for her mother more than he ever revealed to anyone while she was alive.

"Thank you, Mr. Hatcher. You are a kind man."

"Oh, I almost forgot." Mr. Hatcher reached under the counter and pulled out a folded note. "This is for Mrs. Curtis."

Rosalinda hurried down the middle of the street. She wanted to leave word with Father Palo about Hector's death. But when she arrived, she only found a laborer fixing the church roof. He was not a townsman and could not provide much information about the priest's whereabouts. She went inside, hurriedly scratched a note, and then carefully placed it on the altar table where he would be sure to see it.

Rosalinda turned to walk out, but suddenly stopped and returned to the altar. She kneeled saying a prayer that began with,

"Please forgive me Father for feeling joy in the death of Hector," then ending with, "Thank you, thank you, thank you, Amen."

Though not in her original plans for the day, Rosalinda returned home to take stock of things. The garden, showing signs of strain, would survive, as well as the chickens and the goats. She made a mental note to ask Silas about Hector's horse. The burro was fine for an occasional trip. She did not want to use Earl's horse unless it was for chores directly associated with tending to Hattie or the ranch. With her own horse, it will be much easier for frequent trips between Hattie's homestead, the town, and now, her own place.

She made another mental note to go to the assessor's office to ensure that the deed was free of encumbrances. She remembered her mother saying that the property was hers before she married Hector. If the title had not been changed, then there is no chance for Hector's brother Reynaldo to lay claim. Nevertheless, she would need to check on this as soon as possible.

She quickly fed and watered the animals with an extra measure of food. If Hattie were to have complications, her animals would still be all right.

Soon life would be good; excellent in fact. Reflecting on this, she looked over her property before coaxing the burro to step ahead.

A breeze picked up causing her hair to blow across her face. "We best hurry; it looks like those clouds are ready to burst."

She arrived at Hattie's place by noon. As soon as she was done unloading and had given the burro his feed, it started to rain. "One more gift from God." she thought and darted back to the house.

Seeing Hattie sitting in the main room, she immediately told her what she learned from the deputy and leaving a note for the priest. Rosalinda beamed as she recounted each detail.

She unconsciously took both of Hattie's hands in hers. "Do you know what this means?" she said, smiling broadly, not really expecting an answer.

Hattie's face turned glum; her eyes turned down. This caught Rosalinda quite off guard.

She pulled a chair up next to Hattie and patiently waited.

"This means you will be leaving."

It never crossed Rosalinda's mind that she would stop helping Hattie. In the short time she had spent with her, she knew that Hattie was special to her. She was drawn to her like no one else before her; without thought, without reservation. Rosalinda felt a stirring in her heart as she looked at Hattie whose face was suddenly saddened with the possibility of her leaving. But Hattie's dismay could just as well be from the thought of being left alone. But was there something else she's saying with her eyes?

Rosalinda felt nervous and confused but quickly composed herself and looked directly into Hattie's sad eyes. She then leaned forward and said, "I'm in no rush to go anywhere so you can just get those silly thoughts out of your head."

After the supper dishes were washed and Shakespeare fed, Rosalinda went outside to fetch a load of firewood for tomorrow morning. When she returned to the house, the rain on the roof quickly turned from drops to a continuous shower. Despite her emotional challenges of these past days, it felt good to be here, it felt good to be alive. She knelt and loaded the pieces into the kindling box and then threw an extra piece of wood into the stove.

Hattie sat across the room softly rubbing her very large belly and humming a nondescript tune. She gently rocked herself as if she were already holding the baby. Hattie glanced up to watch Rosalinda fiddle with the stove when she noticed a piece of paper nearly falling out from Rosalinda's pocket.

"You're going to drop that piece of paper."

Rosalinda straightened up. "What paper?"

"There, sticking out of your pocket."

Rosalinda felt her pocket. "Oh, my gosh! I'm sorry. I'm really, really sorry. I completely forgot about it. This is yours. I was so wrapped up with my own affairs." She handed it to Hattie then turned away making herself busy with nothing in particular. Hattie glanced at the folded paper then warily made her way to the bedroom to read the letter in private.

Suddenly, with the fury of a mad woman, Hattie burst from the bedroom and propelled herself out of the house. She made it as far as the pump and steadied herself against it with one hand and holding her belly with the other.

The rain was now pummeling the ground splashing mud up onto her ankles. "Damn you, Earl," she shouted into the wind. "You're a coward. You're a liar. You're …"

Just then a great spasm in her belly wrenched the words away from her lips. As she fell, Rosalinda caught her just in time to prevent her from landing hard. But now they were both on the ground. Hattie regained just enough mindfulness to understand that Rosalinda was holding her, and she was now in dire circumstances.

"I'm sorry Rosalinda." She began to sob but was overcome by another wave of pain, groaning, and gasping in agony.

They were both soaked through to the skin, and the thunder rolled over and over as if echoing Hattie's plight. Shakespeare came out of his shelter circling them. He whined in frustration at his inability to help.

Just lifting Hattie's pregnant body from her position on the slippery ground would challenge even the toughest man. By now Hattie's garments were fully drenched and weighed heavily on her frame.

Rosalinda whispered, "Please God I can do this, please God, I can do this." In one great explosion of strength, Rosalinda let out a yell from the depth of her being and lifted Hattie into her arms. With sheer will-power she placed one foot in front of the

other as huge drops of rain pelted her. Hattie wrapped her arms around Rosalinda's neck and held her as tight as her fading strength allowed.

Once inside Rosalinda quickly laid Hattie down then hurried to add more wood to the stove. She put on a pot of water just in case this was not a false alarm.

Hattie had another wave of pain, even harder this time. Rosalinda's hopes of false labor quickly dissipated.

"I'm going to get you out of these wet clothes and make you as comfortable as we can," she said as she washed the mud from her hands and arms in the basin. Rosalinda disappeared momentarily into the next room then reappeared pulling a clean shirt over her head. Next, she threw out the dirty water, rinsed it, and refilled it with clean warm water.

She placed the basin and wash cloth near the bed. "All right then, let's get these off."

Like a skilled nurse, Rosalinda had Hattie washed, in clean linens and a sleeping gown in a matter of minutes. Thankfully, the contractions subsided enough for her to work. She unrolled a piece of white fabric on top of the wooden dresser and uncovered the few surgical tools Dr. Pierce gave her; gauze, bandages, needle, thread, scissors, and string.

She remembered the doctor showing her and her mother how to sterilize the tools. Dr. Pierce was proud to teach his eager assistants this relatively new procedure. It was nearly unheard of in rural areas. He also taught them that if they couldn't boil the

tools, then hold a flame under them, or pour strong alcohol on them.

She placed all the instruments in the boiling pot then carefully placed them on a larger piece of clean gauze. Rosalinda had assisted both her mother and Dr. Pierce with birthing children before, but never for someone she had grown to care for so deeply.

Hattie was screaming again. There was no time to waste.

The rain stopped at some point before dawn but no one, save the birds gorging on half-drowned worms, noticed.

Rosalinda had somehow managed to just fall asleep when she heard a horse pulling a wagon. "Whoa." The voice was familiar. Rosalinda got up and opened the door.

"Holy smoke," Dr. Pierce remarked, "You look like the deaf-mute who spent a week in a well yelling for help."

"Shhhh!" Rosalinda stepped outside.

"Hattie gave birth last night. They're sleeping now. It was difficult, but everyone made it through. Come in, and I'll put on some coffee. You'll probably want to do an examination while you're here."

"Well isn't that something. Did she have a boy or a girl?"

"Both."

"Both?" Dr. Pierce asked. "Hmm, I guess I didn't catch the second heartbeat. You know it's probably a blessing that she didn't make it to full term, you know, the babies being smaller." He pulled up a chair and sat down. "Multiple births can be very tricky even for us doctors. Someone upstairs must have been watching over you two last night."

"You've got that right." Rosalinda remarked and then softly repeated, "You've got that right."

Hattie and the babies began to stir prompting the doctor to go in and perform his duties. When the coffee was ready, Rosalinda took two cups from the shelf but decided to pour the doctor his cup when he was done. It was only then that she noticed the crumpled piece of paper Hattie had dropped on the floor last night. She sat down, sipped her coffee, and read the letter.

The doctor was smiling when he emerged from the room. "You did good, real good. I recommend supplementing the babies with some goat's milk though. Hattie's doing well but needs to save some nutrition intake for herself. In fact, some of that goat's milk would be good for her too. When I get back to town, I'll see if I can get someone to bring one of your goats over."

"My goats! Where has my mind been? I didn't see them at our place when I was there yesterday. Doctor, I have no idea where they are."

"Don't worry. After you left, I asked Silas to take them over to your neighbor for safekeeping and milking. I'm sure they appreciated the free milk in exchange for boarding. I'm sorry I forgot to mention it; must be getting a little old."

Rosalinda handed him a cup of coffee and then placed the letter in front of him.

"What's this?" he asked.

She spoke softly, "It's from her husband. Right after she read it she got extremely upset and went into labor."

He quickly read the short page. "Poor girl; some men get married on a whim and then do everything they can to legitimately not be there. This sounds like it could fester into one of those cases."

Rosalinda noted his words sounded like a prognosis. What she really wanted to know was how all this would affect Hattie.

"Do you think this might slow her recovery?"

"It very well could. Some women get very melancholy after giving birth. I know you're going to be awfully busy but try to give her as much companionship as you can spare. Well I best be off. I was on my way to see the Miller boy."

"Listen, Dr. Pierce would you mind asking the deputy about Hector's horse. It would sure make my trips back and forth much easier."

"I understand. Sure, glad to do it."

He paused at the door and turned back around, "You know, I was just thinking that Esperanza's little girl, Lourdes, might be available to help you out for a while."

"Actually, Esperanza asked me two weeks ago if she could buy a couple of laying hens from my flock, but I was still figuring out how to do it under Hector's nose. I'd be glad to trade chickens and a little money for the extra pair of hands."

"Don't you think that the Curtis's should pay for the girl?

"No sense in worrying about that now. I can spare a few hens."

The doctor nodded in agreement.

"Esperanza is coming by to pick up my laundry this afternoon. I can discuss it with her then. Meanwhile, I'll send someone to fetch one of your goats. Or would you like all three of them?"

Rosalinda thought a moment about her neighbor's four children, "No, I think that one would be good. They can hold on to the two for a while for their kindness."

"Your mother would be proud of you. Your mother and Esperanza were great friends, weren't they? For weeks after your mother's death, I half expected him or Reynaldo, to be found dead by mysterious means after Reynaldo backed up Hector's alibi."

The doctor walked out and climbed to the wagon seat.

"Thank you very much, Dr. Pierce."

He waved back with his hat as he made the turn north towards the Miller's place.

Rosalinda went in to check on Hattie before attending to anything else. She was struggling in her attempts to breastfeed both babies at the same time.

"Here, let me help you." Rosalinda picked up one of the newborns and cradled it in her arms. "Go ahead and feed that one first while I hold this one."

The baby didn't seem to know what to do, and a worried expression fell on Hattie's face.

"Give it a little time," Rosalinda said in a soft assuring tone.

After several futile minutes, Rosalinda went to the kitchen. Hattie heard her movements but could not tell what she was doing. In a few moments she returned with a bowl with a small amount of clear liquid and a piece of white gauze.

"Listen, I'm going to wet your nipple a little with this and we'll see if we can stir up some interest. Is that all right?"

She nodded and then Rosalinda dipped a corner of the gauze in the bowl and gently moistened her nipple with the liquid. Hattie then positioned her nipple into the baby's mouth and the baby began to suckle instantaneously.

"Oh, Thank God." Hattie sighed in relief. "What's in the bowl?"

"Sugar water," Rosalinda set down the bowl. "It doesn't always work, but sometimes the baby's taste buds perk up enough to look for the source. We won't need to do this again, now that the lesson was learned."

Rosalinda sat back into the chair, gently rocking the delicate bundle in her arms. "Have you decided on their names yet?"

"The one in your arms is Clayton. Earl was firm that a boy would be named after his father. His middle name is Leroy; after a friend he had back in Texas."

"And the girl..." Rosalinda asked, "What's her name?"

"Earl said I could pick the name if I had a girl. I always liked the name Martha. So, her first name is Martha."

"And what is her middle name?"

"Rose."

Chapter Ten – Ladies and Gentlemen

After a few days, things started to settle into a comfortable routine. Hattie's strength was steadily building. The infants were thriving on breast milk and the supplemental goat milk Rosalinda fed them while Hattie slept.

Lourdes eagerly helped with the infants. At the age of twelve, she had a strong sense of responsibility, but she was enough of a child to laugh unreservedly at Shakespeare romping after a bothersome horsefly or trying to mimic the distant howl of a coyote.

Hattie sat outside and wrote letters to her mother and Earl. She let her mother know they were now grandparents of a boy and girl. Rosalinda would drop off Earl's letter at the railroad office for the next time someone was riding out to the survey team. This letter was as compassionate as Earl's had been.

Earl

You are a father of two healthy children, Clayton and Martha. We are fine.

Hattie

She had thought to add "No thanks to you" after "we are fine," but decided to leave it be. At the moment, life was good. In fact, she was feeling quite happy.

She knew she should still be furious with Earl, but the anger substantially diminished somewhere between her running outside in the storm and the birth of her children. Trying to remember that night was like trying to remember a dream. She felt some of the dream was real, but how much was her imagination simply filling in the blanks?

When Rosalinda was ready to leave, Hattie handed her the letter and then watched her mount the burro.

"I'll be back as soon as I can." Rosalinda gave Hattie a broad smile which Hattie gave back in return.

After traveling for several minutes, Rosalinda felt a need to stop, turn, and look back. She was sure there was nothing to worry about, and there was nothing that she had forgotten to bring or do; she simply had to look.

From here she could make out that Hattie was still outside and was now giving her a friendly wave. Rosalinda waved back and disappeared down into the wash. It was only a wave, but it made her feel noticeably lighter and prompted her to encourage the burro to move along a bit faster.

To her great surprise, Silas had Hector's horse tethered behind the building. "Silas, how did you manage to get the horse here so quickly?"

"Well, it seems that one of the Logan town officials was going to pass through here and thought that it would be a good idea to have a spare horse. Maybe he had a bad experience once. Who knows? He's a beautiful horse, what's his name?"

Rosalinda responded, "Azufre."

"A-zu-fre, what's that mean?"

"Brimstone, but I call him Zuzu. Hector could barely handle him and said he was the devil's horse, but he's as gentle as a lamb with me."

"Well, I think that says a great deal about Hector and about you. Anyways, I'm glad we were able to get him for you."

"Yes, I'm very grateful. I'll pick him up after I talk with the assessor. Thanks."

The new two-story building towered over the rest of the town. The bank was on the first floor and all the regional government, save the jail, commerce, attorneys, and property-related entities were on the second floor. There were a number of new faces and Rosalinda had to ask twice about who she would need to talk to about her property.

"That would be Mr. Lindsay," answered a man in his early twenties. He seemed a bit put out as he disappeared into an office. On his return he sat down behind his desk and without looking up, pointed to a chair. "Take a seat and we'll let you know when he is available."

For a second Rosalinda wondered who the "We" was since he was the only person there.

From down the hall Rosalinda heard Dr. Pierce's voice. "Rosalinda, there you are; I suspect you haven't talked to Mr. Lindsay yet?"

"No, I haven't. Is there something wrong? Why are you here?"

Just then the office door open and a portly man in a three-piece suit motioned them in. "Please sit down." Mr. Lindsay pointed to the two chairs in front of his desk. "You don't mind if I remove my jacket, do you?" Without waiting for an answer, he removed his jacket and hung it on a coat rack.

Dr. Pierce spoke first. "Rosalinda, I took the liberty of providing Mr. Lindsay with some background information. I also brought your mother's will with me." He reached into the inside pocket of his coat, pulled out the document, and laid it on the desk. It appeared, by the unbroken wax seal, that it had not been read.

"A will? I didn't know my mother had a will."

"Aha. Well." Mr. Lindsay stood up. "Would you excuse me, I'll be right back."

They could hear his leather shoes squeak down the hall and then a mumbled conversation. Rosalinda stared at the document lying on the desk, not saying a word.

A well-dressed, middle-aged man was following Mr. Lindsay. "This is Mr. Benjamin Bowers, Attorney at Large."

"How do you do" Mr. Bowers said as he shook hands with Dr. Pierce and then Rosalinda.

Mr. Lindsay continued, "Dr. Pierce had some suspicions about the will. If Rosalinda's mother left her property to her daughter instead of her second husband, it's probably a good idea to have Ben here present. This is a bit unusual you know."

Rosalinda nervously picked up the document and handed it over to Mr. Bowers.

An hour later Dr. Pierce was pouring brandy into two snifters, "I know it's early in the day for a drink, but this is the only libation I have on hand for a proper toast." He melodramatically cleared his throat, lifted his glass to Rosalinda and pronounced, as if a crowd of fifty were in the room, "Ladies and gentlemen. It brings me the utmost pleasure to introduce you to Miss Rosalinda Garrett, owner of the Garrett Ranch, a stockholder of some measure in Mayer-Becket Pharmaceuticals, and the Standard Oil Company." That said, he tipped his glass towards Rosalinda, and they both savored the moment.

Rosalinda was still smiling yet shaking her head in disbelief. She knew nothing of stocks but knew from Dr. Pierce's reactions that it must all be good. In the reading of the document, she learned that her real father stipulated Rosalinda would receive half of his estate on reaching the age of twenty-one or with the passing of her mother, whichever came first. The other half went directly to her mother. However, her mother kept only a small portion of the assets, and the remaining funds were set up a trust.

Hector never knew, and Dr. Pierce only knew that he was not to open the sealed envelope unless Hector died, or Rosalinda reached her twenty-first birthday.

It would be several weeks before she would know her true net worth. There were bank accounts back east and a parcel of land her father had inherited from his family somewhere in Connecticut. Rosalinda always thought that since her parents did not live like rich people, they probably weren't. Her hopes were growing that there would be enough in all of this for her and Cecelia to live without ever having to be dependent on anyone.

A little later she walked towards the church to talk with Father Palo. Conscious of having liquor on her breath she retrieved a piece of hard candy out of the brown wrapper in her pocket. She rolled it over and over again in her mouth ensuring that her mouth watered with each tumble of the peppermint disks. She covered her head with a scarf, then swallowed several times before entering the open side door to the sanctuary.

When she stepped in, the young priest was trying to kill a wayward bee. Rosalinda remained in the shadows and watched as he deftly jumped, swooped, twirled, and leaped at the bee as if dancing. She had never seen anyone move like that and was captivated. Soon the bee seemed to disappear through an open window, but the priest continued to bounce and twirl. His confessional vestments caught the air like flags flowing in the breeze. Though very odd, what she was witnessing was quite beautiful. She could see he was very strong by the way he would hold a particular position or move in slow motion. Despite his slight stature, his handsome face and gentle eyes both captivated and saddened many a girl who wished he was not a man of the cloth.

Intuitively she knew she was observing a very private matter for the priest and decided to wait awhile outside. She slowly stepped back, but then bumped into a broom. It made a large clapping sound as it hit the tile floor. He looked up, paralyzed with shock.

"I'll come back later Father." She said apologetically.

He caught his breath and raised his hand to shade his eyes trying to get a better focus on the silhouetted figure. "Wait, wait, Rosalinda, I didn't recognize you. For a second, I thought you were Mother Superior Bernadette visiting us from Santa Fe. Oh, what a relief. Please come in. Sit down." He motioned her to the closest pew then took a seat while catching his breath. He could tell that she was still reluctant, and he patted a spot beside him.

Rosalinda sat down, but not too close as she could still taste the brandy through the peppermint. Rosalinda began, "I have some important news for Cecelia."

"Ah, yes I heard that Hector was summoned to face his final judgment. In fact, when I learned that Mrs. Harwell was leaving for Pueblo this morning, I asked her to courier a letter to Father Michaels. I didn't know how soon I would see you and didn't think you would mind. I wrote that it was "Very Urgent on the outside of the letter."

"That's wonderful, Father." Rosalinda said with much relief. "Have you heard any news about Cecelia?"

"No, nothing so far, but I am expecting a package from Father Michaels. Maybe he is sending word with it. You know I heard we will have the telephone here very soon. Too bad we have to wait." He sat back in the pew and gazed up at the wooden carving of Jesus hanging from the cross. Then he said in a confessing tone, "You know, ever since I can remember, I wanted to be a priest. But once, when I was twelve, my mother took me to see a dance troupe." He smiled at Rosalinda and continued, "We were living in St. Louis at the time. My grandmother gave my father the tickets in hopes that he would take my mother to something cultural. Well, a ballet was the last place he would want to be seen, so, my mother took me instead."

Rosalinda was fascinated with his story and felt special to hear something of his past. She nodded and encouraged him with her eyes to go on.

"It was spellbinding. Those men moved and leaped in ways that were as close to flying as a human could without wings. They had to be extremely strong. But they were perfectly proportioned, not bulky and grotesque like the men I've seen loading the river barges. No, these men glided on the stage like angels. Oh, if I could only dance like that; dance like an angel."

The large double doors open in the back of the church. This time it was the Mother Superior.

Rosalinda got up and made the sign of the cross as she left the pew. As she passed the approaching woman, draped in a heavy black habit, Rosalinda lowered her eyes in respect and said, "Good morning Mother Superior."

The nun nodded back in return and briskly walked to the now standing priest. As Rosalinda continued down the aisle she heard the Mother Superior say, "It's a shame that such a young woman would be drinking her way down Satan's path. It's a blessing that she came to you, Father."

By the time Rosalinda reached the deputy's office, Silas had tied the horse out in front of the building. It was a slow day, as were most between paydays, and he was happy for the break in the monotony. He handed her the reins, "Yes, he's a real fine animal, probably the best between here and Taos."

"He's a beauty." She said, rubbing the animal on his nose, his black hair glistening in the sun. Then, she turned towards Silas, "I think my mother died because of him."

"How's that?" he said in surprise.

"Hector was obsessed with him ever since he first laid eyes on him. When he heard that the owner lost nearly everything he owned in a card game Hector drew out all my mother's money to buy him. They had a terrible argument." She drew in a large breath and released it, "When I saw her on the ground in the shed, he came out saying that she got kicked by one of the burros while trying to pull a thorn from its hoof."

"But what about the witnesses? Reynaldo and what's his name, Fernando? I wasn't in town during all of this. I only got things third hand."

"I tried to explain things to the circuit judge, but he didn't believe me. Reynaldo and Fernando were on the other side of the shed loading up the wagon for a cock-fight that night when it happened; they didn't see a thing. Hector told them exactly what to say to the authorities, but I saw Hector washing off the ax handle." She momentarily paused to tether the burro to the horse's saddle. "The judge didn't seem very concerned about the demise of a poor Mexican woman. Dr. Pierce tried to convince him as well, but since he wasn't an eye-witness the judge wouldn't spend any more time on it."

Silas nodded that he understood.

She mounted the horse as if he had always been her animal. She looked concerned and then asked, "Have you seen Reynaldo? I assumed that he was with Hector."

"Oh right, he's going to be a guest of the Logan jail for about a year I suspect. They had charges against from an earlier visit. It was very convenient for the law that someone knocked him out during the brawl."

"That's good. Does his wife know?"

"I heard that she is moving the family to her brother's place in El Paso. Word is that she's hoping he won't bother to follow."

"Thanks for everything Silas."

"So long now. Take care."

Eleven – Legend of Tucumcari Mountain

Mrs. Harwell arrived at Father Michael's church in Pueblo by noon on Wednesday. As she handed the priest the envelope, he apologetically explained that Cecelia found work with a family on their way to San Francisco and had already left.

"Oh dear," Mrs. Harwell said. "Father Palo will be so disappointed. He's such a nice young man. I'll hate to give him this news."

"Don't worry. Cecelia had already written a letter, and we got it off in a package going to Father Palo yesterday. I'm sure things will eventually get sorted out."

Rosalinda focused on tending to Hattie's vegetable garden and her own new section. The fine weather over the past few days created excellent conditions for growing everything, especially the weeds.

With Lourdes doing most of the household chores, Hattie often visited Rosalinda in the garden while the infants slept.

As Hattie watched Rosalinda from a few feet away, she marveled at how efficiently she moved. Each chop of the hoe was

rhythmic. The side-cut movements not only cut the weeds but left neat furrows where the cut weeds between the plants could easily be picked up later.

"Do you mind if I watch you work? I don't want to slow down your progress; you seem quite practiced at it." Hattie then extended a tin cup full of water to her

"Thanks. That was very thoughtful of you." She took the cup and wiped her brow with her forearm.

"When I was small, I used to watch Cassie, my mammy, well now she's my mother's maid, work in our garden at the back of the house. I would follow behind her real quiet like. She knew I was there and after a while, she sang as she worked. Sometimes it almost seemed like she was in a trance or was totally at peace. Does that make sense? I mean, when I watched you work, the way you moved reminded me a little of her."

"It makes perfect sense to me. Sometimes it is trance-like I suppose. Listen, I'm done here for now. Maybe we can sit in the shade of the barn over there." They sat down on the makeshift bench consisting of a plank atop two overturned barrels. They enjoyed the cool wall as they leaned back.

"Ah this feels good. It was getting a little hot out there," Rosalinda said drinking the last of the water.

"Do you want another cup? I'd be happy to draw you another."

"No; but thank you." Rosalinda said as she lifted her cup and nodded as if she just gave her a small toast.

She put the cup down on the bench next to her side, "I followed behind my mother in her garden, and she would hum and sing as well. She said that as she worked, she thought about the people she loved, both here and in heaven. She also said that you should bury your anger in the dirt, so you wouldn't take it inside the house. At first, I didn't believe her. But when I saw how my stepfather mistreated her, instead of turning around and taking it out on my sister and me, she would dig rocks out of a new section, cut a furrow with a hoe that could rival a plow, or pull weeds like she was strangling someone's neck. But, you knew that she'd come back inside and smother us with hugs and kisses."

Hattie's eyes were wide, keenly listening to her every syllable. She noticed how Rosalinda's beautiful hazel eyes squinted as she pondered her thoughts. She never seemed to just let the words fall out of her mouth; she was both deliberate and at ease. She also perceived her eyes to light up to nearly blue when mentioning her mother's affection and how they nearly turned to brown when she was sad; truly a mirror into her soul.

Rosalinda tilted her head toward the garden. "When I got to be old enough, I worked alongside her and found that I too could bury at least some of my anger in the dirt. And now, since my mother died, when I'm really getting into the flow of the work, I can almost feel her right next to me."

Rosalinda paused a moment to watch Shakespeare chase a lizard around a rock. "Maybe Cassie felt her loved ones as she worked, or maybe she just felt right with the world with you close by."

Hattie looked straight ahead and cleared her throat, "Well do you think I could work alongside you tomorrow?" She wasn't sure how Rosalinda would respond so she thought a second and added, "I know I've got a lot of anger burying to do."

"Yes, of course, you can. I'd love your company. But, you've got to promise not to overdo it."

For the next several days Hattie spent every available minute helping Rosalinda with the gardening. Usually, they worked along-side one another so Rosalinda could easily instruct Hattie on how to hold and use various tools. But, it was also the easiest way to talk with one another.

With Hattie's encouragement, Rosalinda talked about what it was like growing up in a town known for shootouts and shady deals. As she finished one story, Hattie tried to tease another one from her. It was like trying to get at the right string to pull open a sack of feed. She always succeeded, but Rosalinda was more than happy to watch Hattie's beautiful eyes light up as she recalled some of the more interesting accounts of the area.

At other times, primarily when Hattie thought she might be getting to be a bother, she quietly worked her row next to Rosalinda's. As the days went by, she found she was enjoying the quiet time nearly as much as when Rosalinda was talking.

Hattie could tell when Rosalinda worked just a little slower, so she could catch up and be near again. Whenever she looked up, Rosalinda was ready with a smile; never trying to make her do more than what she was comfortable with.

Hattie thought about this for a moment. Whenever she fell just the least bit behind Earl, whether it was doing a chore, or even just walking, he'd let his irritation out in some manner. Sometimes he'd impatiently shake his head and let out a theatrical sigh, but more often he would whine, "For God's sake woman, my old granny could move faster than you." Or, he would say "a three-legged turtle, or a "broken-back jackass, or a pile of shit could move faster than you."

Rosalinda noticed that Hattie's hoe was chopping in a frenzied pace. "Whoa up there Hattie, I didn't think we were racing."

Hattie straightened up and turned around to see Rosalinda smiling and resting her chin on her hands atop her hoe handle. She looked a little like one of those three-legged stands used for photography cameras.

"Oh, I didn't realize – I mean I was just thinking about Earl and…"

Rosalinda stepped over into Hattie's row. "I know what you mean, and I approve." She gently touched Hattie's elbow. "This is the perfect place to let loose of your pent-up anger. But make sure you don't accidently chop something you want to keep, or make a furrow going northeast instead of the intended due east. I can't tell you the number of times I've had to correct my course because I was so stirred up over something – most times about my stepfather. I swear if I hadn't had a patch of ground to stick, stab, chop, or hack, I would have taken my rage directly to the source a long time ago. And, that would not have been a good thing."

Rosalinda stepped back over to her own row, smiled, and said, "Now that I know you're leading a charge, I'll just go at my own speed unless you call for reinforcements."

Hattie loved how Rosalinda's smile made her feel; like she was valuable, worthwhile, and unquestionably appreciated just for being herself.

When Rosalinda and Hattie finished cultivating the rows for the day, Rosalinda said, "Well I think that about does it for now. Let's wash up and during supper, I'll tell you a story about that big flat top mountain over there."

While Rosalinda cooked, she could hear Hattie enjoying the company of her children in the next room. As the babies nursed, Hattie told them little stories about fuzzy baby chicks, mama rabbits, Shakespeare trying to catch a fly out by the barn, and Cassie humming to her vegetables.

Soon the children were asleep, and Hattie came out taking a place at the table. Lourdes sat on the other side picking out the stones from the dry beans to be soaked overnight.

"Ahem." Hattie sounded, then playfully tapped her fingers on the table until Rosalinda turned around from the stove.

"Another stir, and it should be ready."

"I can't wait." Hattie said like a little girl waiting for a piece of candy."

"You weren't so excited the last time we had lima beans," Rosalinda sarcastically replied.

Lourdes thought they must have been out in the sun too long and stopped picking at the beans to look up.

Rosalinda filled the bowls, propped a piece of cornbread on the edge of each, and set them on the table.

Hattie bowed her head and said, "Heavenly Father we thank you for this meal and our many blessings. Amen"

"Lourdes" Rosalinda turned to the girl, "Do you remember the story about Tucumcari Mountain?"

"I have heard it in pieces, so I could not tell it very good if you asked me to tell it to you."

"That's all right. I remember how it goes. But you should know that some think it really happened. Others believe it was just made up by a Methodist minister who used to live around here."

"Hold on." Hattie got up and took Rosalinda's bowl. "I'm going to put this over by the stove to keep it warm."

"Thanks. The legend begins with an Apache Indian village on top of the mountain. Their chief, Wautonomah, foresaw his approaching death and was troubled about who he should name as the next chief. One day the chief called Tonopah and Tucum to his side. They were his two finest braves who were deadly enemies and rivals for the hand of his daughter Kari. Kari already

loved Tucum and despised Tonopah, but her father would decide who she would marry.

The chief gathered up the braves, told them that he would soon die, and one of them would succeed him. Wautonomah told them mortal combat with knives would decide and the victor would also claim Kari as his wife."

Hattie and Lourdes both had eyes as bright and wide as eggs about to be flipped over in a skillet.

Rosalinda took a sip of water, "Now that very night, the rivals began their fight to the death, while Kari watched from a hidden spot nearby. They both fought hard, but it was Tonopah's knife piercing Tucum's heart. In agony Kari screamed and rushed forth, plunging her own knife into the surviving brave. And then, in her grief she took her lover's knife from his lifeless hands and stabbed herself. With her last breath, she crumpled atop Tucum's body.

Later, when the chief arrived at the scene, he found that the three dearest people to him were dead. Overwhelmed with sorrow, he took Kari's knife and thrust it into himself. In his dying gasp he uttered "Tucum...Kari." So now we know the mountain as Tucumcari."

There was a pause then Lourdes said, "Rosalinda, you tell this story so much better than I have ever heard it before."

"Thank you, Lourdes, but remember that the story may not be true. It is most likely that the word Tucumcari came from an Indian word. When the Apaches were here it meant "place of the buffalo hunt." Now as you look around the mountain, it just seems to shoot up out of nowhere. I heard it is seven hundred feet high. From up there, I bet the Indians could observe the movement of buffalo and other game quite easily from several vantage points up there. Anyway, you decide for yourself which story you want to believe, and now I'm going to enjoy my lima beans.

Chapter Twelve – Empty Handed

After supper, the two women stepped out to look at the mountain they had seen so many times. But after hearing the legend, they felt an increasing tug hoping the story was based on some truth – the truth that love could be felt so deep and be so profound that life itself could be sacrificed for it.

They continued to gaze at the mountain shading their eyes from the late afternoon sun. Then they noticed some movement in the distance and focused on a black object heading their direction. As it moved closer, they saw it was leaving a small cloud of dust trailing behind.

A moment later Hattie exclaimed, "It's a horseless carriage. Rosalinda, it's an automobile."

Rosalinda responded, "What? Why on earth would one of those things be coming here?"

As it came to a halt in front of the house, the machine whirred, jerked, and let out a pop, pop, pop. After a second the door opened, and Ben Bowers stepped out. The other door opened, and Father Palo struggled to find his balance. Inside the house, Lourdes tried to calm the obviously upset babies while, at the same time, tried to see what was going on.

Mr. Bowers spoke first, "I'm sorry about that, ladies." He pointed his leather cap in the direction of the machine, "My little Lizzy here can be a bit testy at times."

Rosalinda wondered what it was about this machine that made it female. Was it because the machine was difficult to handle so it must be 'testy' and therefore a female? She shook this train of thought from her head.

Hattie loved the surprise company but reserved her feelings until she knew the nature of their call.

Father Palo took out an envelope and handed it to Rosalinda. "It's from your sister. It came with that package I was expecting from Father Michaels."

"Thank you, Father. I appreciate you coming out all this way."

Hattie and Rosalinda both looked at Mr. Bowers as if asking him to explain his appearance.

"Oh, uh, I just offered to give our young Father here a lift. I don't have any news on your estate; hopefully we'll hear something in a couple of weeks, maybe sooner from the banks back East."

Hattie asked, "Would you like a cup of coffee? It'll only take a minute to get it going." But she had just heard something she couldn't understand; estate? What estate?

Mr. Bowers answered, "Oh no thank you. We've got a few more places to stop before heading back."

Father Palo stepped back up into the automobile and pulled the door shut while Mr. Bowers bent over to crank the machine to life. Again, it gave a pop but quickly settled into a rhythmic beat. He hopped in and left as quickly as they came.

Hattie watched them disappear as Rosalinda sat down in the shade of the porch and opened her letter.

> *Rosalinda, My Dear Sister,*
>
> *I have found work with a kind family. They are going to settle in San Francisco and have hired me to help take care of their four children. The father was promoted to a high position with a shipping company and can now afford the added help. The family name is Herman. The father's name is Aster and the mother is Annabelle. Their address is 210 Presidio Boulevard, San Francisco.*
>
> *While my heart aches to leave you, I know it is best to be as far away from Hector as possible.*
>
> *Your loving sister, Cecelia*

Rosalinda folded the letter, put it in her pocket, and then walked back to the row of melons where she had left off. Hattie saw by the expression on Rosalinda's face that something in the letter caused a great heaviness on her. Hattie followed her, reached out and softly placed her hand on Rosalinda's forearm.

"Is there's something I can do?" Hattie asked.

Rosalinda simply shook her head, but Hattie already knew there was nothing.

Rosalinda's feelings were ranging from frustration, sadness, anger, and numbness. Nothing would alter the course of her sister's path to California.

At one point she considered mounting her horse in hopes of somehow catching up. But they were already several days out of Pueblo and it would take several days just to reach Pueblo. Thinking it through, she came to her senses and realized that, like most things, the best approach was to plan. But plan what?

Her energies were now being torn in too many directions. There was her own property to take of, an estate to settle, the Curtis ranch, two infants, a borrowed girl, her sister; wherever she was, and Hattie.

Lourdes routinely ate supper with them and then left in time to get home before dark. Tonight, after Lourdes left, Rosalinda replenished the wood by the stove then went out on the porch to be with Shakespeare. Holding his strong head in her two hands, she massaged him behind the ears. He gazed back at her with his dreamy grateful eyes. "You're the only thing in my life that makes sense right now."

She heard Hattie singing softly to the babies who made their last fading attempts to communicate before being comforted to sleep. She envied the simplicity of their existence; to awaken to a world waiting to hold you and feed you; a world, at least for now, that would anticipate and care for your every discomfort. Soon the singing gently stopped, and only the sound of a single cricket penetrated the still air.

Shakespeare decided he needed to scratch himself more instead of the massage, so he moved a few feet away to give his hind foot plenty of swinging space.

Hattie came out to the porch bringing a chair with her. Can I join you?" she asked.

Rosalinda nodded then Hattie positioned the chair next to hers. Rosalinda expected Hattie to say or ask something, but she did not.

They sat for a minute in silence before Rosalinda spoke, "That cricket seems to be making quite a fuss all by himself." She swallowed hard, holding back her tears.

"Maybe that's why he's making all the fuss; because he is by himself." Hattie softly said. She then placed her hand gently on Rosalinda's.

Tears began to leak from Rosalinda's eyes that were staring out at the rising moon. With her free hand, she pulled out Cecelia's letter and handed it to Hattie. She struggled to read it by the light from the house, but she could not make out anything on the paper.

Rosalinda didn't wait for her to finish reading the letter. "She's on her way to San Francisco. I can't stop her; they've got too much of a head start. I can't think of what to do; my brain is as stuck as that jar of peaches I tried to open this morning, and it never budged." She turned slightly towards Hattie, "You didn't

157

know you were supposed to have peaches this morning, did you?"

Hattie squeezed her hand, gave a conciliatory smile, and shook her head, no. It pained Hattie deeply to see Rosalinda in such distress and was now resisting a sudden and inexplicable desire to surround Rosalinda in her arms. How she wished she could take away her pain.

Rosalinda's nose was now running terribly so Hattie pulled out a rumpled handkerchief from her sleeve and held it out, "I can get you a fresh one if you like."

Rosalinda took the handkerchief with her one free hand and awkwardly blew into it. Hattie realized that she was relieved when Rosalinda decided to continue holding her hand. After some hesitation, Hattie gently placed her other hand on Rosalinda's as well. She looked at Rosalinda for any signs of resistance and then tenderly began to stroke Rosalinda's hand.

Rosalinda felt her face begin to flush and her heart quicken. She was suddenly aware that Hattie might be able to see the effect her simple act of kindness had on her. Her mind was telling her to pull her hand away, but her heart was deliriously trapped, and she savored this one precious moment.

It was as if every fiber of her body needed this. It was like the way seeds burst out from the earth when the sun and rain command them to live – to push through the crust and demand its rightful place on God's planet. This was that moment. She wanted to take her place on this earth.

But then, a great iron gate started to close within her, trapping her with painful doubts; protecting her from uncertainty. The fleeting moment of joy was now turning to fear. She must hide her attraction to Hattie, but how? Her heart was heavy with this new sadness, and another wave of tears welled up again, spilling silently down her face.

"We'll figure something out." Hattie consoled, "Things always look better in the morning." Hattie's words felt so inadequate and trite that she almost wished she hadn't said them. Now Rosalinda was crying even more, maybe she made things worse.

"I'm sorry. That sounded stupid. But we will think of something; I know we will."

Shakespeare ran off and disappeared behind the barn and found something that was worth barking about.

Rosalinda took away her hand and said, "I better find out what he's upset about. It could be something I wouldn't want him to mess with." Without looking back at Hattie, she got up, fully blew into the handkerchief with both hands and then walked away.

Rosalinda did not return to the house until she was certain that Hattie had gone to bed. Shakespeare's ruckus was only a show of stubbornness between himself and a raccoon looking for a meal of fresh eggs. In the end the raccoon fled, empty-handed.

She quietly undressed and slipped under her bedcovers. The moon was high and cast a soft blue light through the window. Rosalinda held up her hand that was so gently held by Hattie. She examined it for a moment, turning it slowing back and forth. As she lowered it back to her chest, she exhaled and silently mouthed the words of her crestfallen epitome, "Empty... handed.

Chapter Thirteen – Pale Blue Ribbon

As usual, Lourdes showed up about an hour after sunrise. By then Rosalinda had already finished milking the goats and fed all the animals. She needed to go to her property today to take care of a few things and looked forward to being away from the Curtis ranch, if only for a few hours. She had not talked to Hattie this morning and didn't want to.

She brought a portion of the milk into the house and handed over the galvanized milk can to Lourdes. Rosalinda then turned towards the open door intending to carry the rest of the milk down to the cool root cellar. When she stepped outside, she was surprised to hear Mr. Bowers' automobile. In a few minutes it pulled up to the front of the house, and again Father Palo was in the passenger seat.

Mr. Bowers was smiling and started talking before he was quite out of the vehicle, "Hello Rosalinda. We got tied up at our last stop and had to spend the night."

Father Palo, also in a very good mood, closed the door behind him and stepped towards Rosalinda. She was very puzzled by their cheerfulness and said, "Would you like to come in for some coffee?"

"Yes, we would, wouldn't you Father?"

Hattie, overhearing, was already reheating the coffee on the stove.

"It looks like it's going to be a fine day." Father Palo said with a grin.

The kitchen only had two chairs, so Ben retrieved the other two from the porch.

They all sat down, and Hattie placed cups of coffee in front of the men.

Father Palo took a small sip then said, "We had this idea last night. We almost didn't wait for sunrise." The men looked at each other like two conniving school boys. "Anyway, Father Michaels left me a note in the package as well as explaining the circumstances of the letter from your sister. And, well the two of us have been trying to figure out what, if anything, we could do to get word to Cecelia." Ben was bobbing his head in agreement.

"You tell it, Ben."

Rosalinda was looking back and forth between the two men so quickly she was feeling a bit dizzy.

Ben swallowed the coffee wiping his lips with the back of his hand. "Well, we can't get word to her immediately. But," he continued," I have a brother who has a law firm in San Francisco. I can wire him today about talking with someone at the shipping company where Mr. Herman works. They may know the route the family is taking. If he got a big promotion, chances are the company is paying to move the family. So, if they are paying, they probably know his route. There can only be so many 'Aster Herman's' working in the shipping business."

"And," Father Palo interrupted, "If part of the journey is by train, we can easily send a wire ahead to the ticketing office where they will board!"

"That's wonderful!" Hattie nearly squealed, patting her own cheeks with joy. "Rosalinda, you see, things really do look better in the morning."

Rosalinda left on horseback for town shortly after the men left. Due to the lack of good roads, and using her shortcuts, she would get there before them.

Hattie walked out a ways watching Rosalinda ride to the rise at the south end of the ranch. Hattie's heart felt heavy and unsettled. This morning's news should have caused Rosalinda great elation, but it didn't. There was genuine relief in Rosalinda's expressions, and she looked truly grateful, but why didn't she look happy?

Did Rosalinda's coolness have anything to do with her holding Rosalinda's hand last night? She couldn't help but think about it. Maybe Rosalinda wasn't someone who could share her tears with anyone, and she was embarrassed. Or maybe Rosalinda sensed there was something beyond the simple act of kindness, because there was; wasn't there? Now she was even more confused. Where on earth was her mind going with this line of thought?

Hattie didn't need her cane anymore but found she often carried it about when she wasn't tending to a baby or doing a chore. Now, as she caught the last glimpse of Rosalinda, she held it to her chest, gently rubbing the soft rabbit fur and worried.

Rosalina arrived in town before the automobile, so she went on to Hatcher's store. There she purchased almost half of a pound of peppermint candy and lemon drops.

"Having a party are yeh?" Mr. Hatcher asked as he poured the candy into a paper bag. Rosalinda was distant and didn't answer. "You all right darlin'? Anything I can do for you?"

Rosalinda snapped back to the present conversation, "Oh, I'm sorry, I'm fine. I just have a lot on my mind these days."

"Well," Mr. Hatcher said, handing her the bag, "just don't eat all of this at once. A belly ache won't help you think any better."

Rosalinda looked over at the large roll of brown wrapping paper. "Would you mind tearing off a small piece of paper and letting me borrow a pencil?"

"Be happy to." He said. He tore off several inches from the roll and then gave her the pencil from the back of his ear.

"Thanks," she said and went outside. She sat down on the long wooden bench; a favorite spot where the community's

elderly men exchanged stories and gossip. Fortunately, this time of day was a bit early for them to gather, leaving Rosalinda alone while she drafted the telegraph to Cecelia.

CECELIA, HECTOR IS DEAD. REYNALDO IN JAIL. SAFE TO COME HOME. I CAN SEND MONEY. LOVE ROSALINDA

She met up with Father Palo and Ben Bowers at the telegraph office, located next to the railroad office. She momentarily fantasized about getting on a train to join Cecelia, but she couldn't just leave.

Ben handed the completed form to the clerk. The telegram, addressed to his brother in San Francisco, included instructions and a message from Rosalinda. He was to forward it as soon as he located the Herman family. Once the clerk read the message and calculated the charges, Ben paid the man and began to turn away.

"Oh Mr. Bowers," the clerk said, "Don't leave, a message came in for you earlier today. Those businessmen back east got a few hours jump start on us. Here you go." He took the message to where Rosalinda and Father Palo were waiting outside.

"I got a telegram here from one of the banks holding Rosalinda's assets. Let's go on over to my office." Smiling at Father Palo he said, "Now Johnny, I know you'd love to know what the telegram says, but I would never eavesdrop on one of your confessionals. I'll see you later tonight for dinner."

At his office, Ben motioned for Rosalinda to take a seat and then sat behind his desk. "Well, at least I know I'll get paid for my services," he said and then handed over the telegram.

Rosalinda read it quickly. Her astonishment was the same as when heard she had any assets at all. She read it once again.

MR. BENJAMIN BOWERS ESQUIRE.

ESTATE MATTER UNDERSTOOD. NO NEED TO PROBATE THIS ACCOUNT, ASSETS HELD IN JOINT TENANCY. FIVE HUNDRED DOLLARS WIRED FOR YOUR CLIENT TO TUCUMCARI BANK PER YOUR REQUEST. LETTER TO FOLLOW WITH ACCOUNT DETAILS.

PLEASE PROVIDE DISPOSITION INSTRUCTIONS OF THE REMAINING $60,185.79 CASH AT YOUR EARLIEST CONVENIENCE. THERE IS A SAFE DEPOSIT BOX, STOCK SHARES, BONDS, AND PROPERTIES TO BE CONSIDERED AS WELL.

CONTACT MR. JAMES DORCHESTER ESQUIRE ON THAT REGARD.

Five hundred dollars was a huge sum of money; sixty thousand was enormous! She looked up at Ben, "That's probably more than a school teacher makes in a lifetime."

"I'd say at least that. My cousin in Chicago is the head of the city's accounting department, and he makes $4,000 a year. Now, take some advice. When you acquire so much money at once scoundrels pop up out of nowhere. And, they are very good at seeing to it that you have nothing to show for it. Now I want you to memorize these words, 'I have an attorney on retainer.' Now say it with me."

"I have an attorney on retainer." They said in unison.

"But what does it mean?" she asked.

"Before you contemplate becoming a party to any deal, you tell whoever it is that you have an attorney on retainer. The vast majority of snakes and vultures will back off. It means you have an established attorney-client relationship. Before making any commitments, you intend to have all your legal matters reviewed by your attorney. "He paused for a moment, "This assumes, of course, that you want to retain a lawyer, and I hope that you will consider retaining me."

Rosalinda was still considering what he had just said.

"You can, of course, sever this relationship at any time."

"Do I have to sign or do anything? I would think there would be a fee. I'd be happy to have you on retainer. Is that the right way to say it?"

"Yes, that's right. I'd say two dollars is adequate, and you won't have to pay it again. If you need anything reviewed, I'll tell you up front what the fees would be."

Rosalinda nodded her consent and then reached into her small satchel. She placed two one-dollar coins on his desk. Then, he carefully entered the amount into a leather-bound book of green pages with columns.

He stood up and shook her hand. "There, that's all there is to it."

She stood up as well and said, "Well, my life is turning out to be very different than I ever imagined a month ago. Thank you for your advice."

"You're welcome. That's what I'm here for."

As she walked to the bank she caught a glimpse of herself in the window of Steinman's Mercantile store. Suddenly she became aware of her clothes. Her blouse had been mended several times, twice at the seams behind her armpits, and once at her right elbow. She never gave much thought to her garments; they were purely functional.

Most people knew she was poor and she rarely had much call to mingle with those who were not, save Dr. Pierce and a few of his clients when he needed her assistance. But now as she looked at herself, the thought of walking into the bank looking not much better than a pauper was not suitable.

Mr. Steinman, somewhere in the back, called to his wife in the front, "I can't find it. Where did you say it was?"

Mrs. Steinman heard the jingle of the door as Rosalinda walked in, "I'll be with you momentarily. I just have to attend to Mr. Steinman for a minute."

Rosalinda moved towards the ready-made clothing. It had been years since she had anything new and those garments were homemade. She noticed the clothing had assorted sizes but didn't know her size. She also didn't know what to buy. She calculated that with the one dollar and thirty-five cents she had left in her satchel; she would buy just enough to be presentable.

Mrs. Steinman came fluttering back. "Men – sometimes you wonder how they can live a day without a woman's guidance. Well now, how have you been? We haven't seen you since last spring when young David decided to paint your burro while you helped the doctor with our Sarah."

Rosalinda laughed, "Oh yes, I remember – that was pretty funny. We walked out onto your front porch, and my burro had turned into a zebra. You know the hardest part was not to laugh until your husband took David out of sight."

Rosalinda scanned the neat stacks of folded blouses. The store primarily stocked practical work clothes and church attire because there was very little call for fancy garments. Still, to Rosalinda, the selection seemed vast.

"Are you looking for something in particular today?" Mrs. Steinman asked.

Rosalinda looked up from a pale blue blouse that had caught her eye. "I have some business to attend to at the bank and, well, I thought I should…"

Mrs. Steinman didn't wait for her to finish, "Ah yes, that blouse you were just looking at would do." She then motioned to the end of the shelf, "and this, you might consider as well."

It was perfect. It was also pale blue, but this one was pin-striped in gray, with mother of pearl buttons, and a high white lace collar adorned with a smart black velvet ribbon tie.

"Yes, I like that one very much."

"You can try it on if you like, but I'm pretty sure it will fit. Would you also be wanting a skirt today?"

"Perhaps later, I'm afraid that I only have a little over one dollar on me right now."

Mrs. Steinman thought for a second, "I have a skirt that was returned because it had a split seam. I fixed it, but I can't sell it as new. Let's see if it fits. Go ahead, step behind the screen, and put on the blouse. I'll fetch the skirt."

Mrs. Steinman seemed quite pleased with herself and as she started to walk away added, "I'll get you a matching ribbon for your hair while I'm at it."

Mrs. Steinman returned in a minute with the items; a pale blue ribbon and a fine charcoal gray skirt. "When you're done honey, come out and see how you look in the mirror here."

After a few minutes, Rosalinda sheepishly stepped out from behind the changing screen. She walked over towards

Mrs. Steinman who was standing in front of an oval-shaped full-length mirror.

"Why they fit perfectly. Come look." She said and stepped to the side.

Rosalinda almost thought she was looking at someone else; perhaps her mother as she remembered her when her father was still alive. She faintly remembered how beautiful she was.

"So, how do you like the skirt? Do you feel comfortable?"

"Oh uh, everything's perfect. Are you sure I have enough money?"

Mrs. Steinman put her hands on her hips smiling, "Well everything you have so far comes to ninety-five cents, so you have more than enough."

"Thank you. Thank you very much."

Mrs. Steinman looked towards the changing screen. "What would you like me to do with your old clothes?"

"If you don't mind, I'll pick them up when I'm done at the bank."

"No, I don't mind at all. I'll have them for you behind the counter."

As Rosalinda approached the bank, she realized she was barely breathing. "This is silly," she thought to herself and then took in three full breaths. The conversation with herself

continued, "This is not a bad thing. There is nothing to fear. After all, I already have a savings account of two dollars that my mother set up for me. That's a lot of money. It would take days for the average man to earn that much." She took in one more large breath and went in.

There was one teller behind an ornate wrought-iron barrier. One man was being helped and another stood in the queue behind him. Rosalinda then stood in line behind him.

She was still silently talking to herself when suddenly the man in front of her took a large step backwards to sneeze. He accidentally bumped into her, nearly toppling her over.

"I'm terribly sorry madam. Please excuse my unintentional, yet quite rude behavior. I do hope you're quite all right."

"Why yes, I'm perfectly fine. Don't think a thing more about it."

"Thank you, ma'am." He said, tipped his head down then turned back to the now free teller.

Amazed, Rosalinda quickly glanced around the room to see if anyone witnessed the incident. Surely, they would point and snicker, if they saw the exchange. But no one was pointing, sneering, gawking, or making any unusual movements. Then it hit her. It hit her as squarely as a bird flying into a glass window. She whispered, "They don't recognize me. They don't know who I am." Then she thought, "That man didn't know he bumped into a woman from the poor end of town."

The teller was now free, and Rosalinda stepped up to the window.

"Yes ma'am, how may I help you today?" the teller took a second look. "Rosalinda, I'm sorry, I didn't recognize you."

"Hello, Mathew," Rosalinda responded, feeling a blush on her cheeks.

The tall, skinny man just stood staring for a second then swallowed, causing his Adam's apple to float up and down like a fishing bobber. Finally, he snapped to and said, "Uh, Mr. Hanover is expecting you. Why don't you take a chair over there and I'll let him know you're here."

He closed his window and then walked over to Mr. Hanover's open office door. He knocked, leaned his head inside, and then backed out of his employer's way.

Mr. Hanover stepped out, smiled at Rosalinda in a gentlemanly manner, and said, "Please come in. We've been anticipating your visit."

Rosalinda wondered if anyone else was in his office, but found he was the only one there.

Rosalinda returned to the mercantile store thirty minutes later. With a little over four hundred dollars in her account and fifty dollars in her satchel, she decided to purchase some sorely needed work clothes. She would not let this windfall money go to

her head. She figured that someone in her family worked hard for it, and so decided she would not spend it like a child.

She selected three men's shirts, one pair of work trousers, and a pair of coveralls. She stacked them on the counter where Mrs. Steinman was patiently waiting.

Rosalinda patted the clothes in indecision.

"Would there be anything else for you today?"

Rosalinda turned slowly as if the shelves in the back corner were calling her name. From her vantage point, Mrs. Steinman, could not see where Rosalinda was looking so she began to fold Rosalinda's selections into a neat pile.

When Rosalinda returned to the counter, she added several dozen soft cloth diapers, baby gowns, and another set of work clothes, only a size smaller.

"Are you sure you want the smaller size as well?"

Rosalinda simply replied, "Yes, these are fine."

When she stepped outside into the bright late morning sun, Ben Bowers happened by in his Oldsmobile Dash Runabout.

"Ben, Ben!" she called out, stretching her head above her parcels, hoping to get his attention.

He maneuvered his vehicle out of the thoroughfare and stopped.

"My, my," he said, "You look like a lady with money in her pockets or used to have money in her pockets. Where're you off to?"

Ben observed Rosalinda as she struggled with her load. "Would you like a ride or at least give your packages a ride somewhere?" he asked while stepping forward to reach for the packages.

"I'm afraid I didn't think this through this very well. I was hoping to borrow Mr. Hatcher's rig for my horse to pull."

"Well you could, but you don't need to. And with you all gussied up you'd probably want to change back into your old clothes before getting up in the saddle." Ben placed her packages behind the seats. "Now, do you need to stop anywhere else?"

Rosalinda realized that riding in his vehicle would be the best option and she was grateful for the offer.

Rosalinda replied, "If you don't mind, I'd like to pick up some things at Hatcher's store. Afterward, we'll need to tether a line off your machine here for the horse."

"That sounds fine," he said, then walked around to open the passenger door.

Chapter Fourteen – No, Not Fine

Hattie gathered the soiled diapers and placed them outside next to a large galvanized bucket. Soon Lourdes would wash and then hang them up to dry. Fortunately, the constant breeze dries them very quickly and are ready by the time the babies need to be changed. Hattie was grateful that Rosalinda fashioned half a dozen diapers out of Earl's long johns, but six diapers for two bottoms was proving to be a challenge.

Lourdes busily tended the fire under the big pot to boil the diapers. Hattie gazed in vain towards the hill where she last saw Rosalinda and her horse disappear and where she hoped Rosalinda would soon return.

Hattie was confused – why didn't Rosalinda's mood change to joy when she learned her sister would get word within a couple of days? Was she having second thoughts about staying on? Or, did she sense something else when I held her hand? She struggled with this last thought over and over again. All she could do was wait and see if she could read even the slightest indications in Rosalinda's voice or demeanor. No matter what; the waiting and speculating was awful.

She felt antsy and decided it was better to keep busy, so she fetched another bucket of water for Lourdes. She already checked

on the children and both were comfortably settled, and so now she headed towards the barn.

"Señora," Lourdes called out towards her, "I already did the milking."

Hattie sighed in disappointment and turned around. She hoped the task of milking would soothe her anxiousness.

Hattie sat down for a few moments on the large stump used for chopping wood. The morning sun bathed her face, and it felt good. But she did not feel quite together, kind of like an untied shoelace. She glanced towards the garden and headed in that direction.

Walking along its length, Hattie saw that Rosalinda had carefully tended to her original garden, even though she had one of her own. In fact, each plant now had a meticulously-shaped earthen mound or a ring, depending on the plant type. She remembered that when she sowed the seeds, she thought that just getting them in a row was all that would be needed. Now there were furrows for irrigation and straw around the bases of the tender plants. Now there was planning and order, very different from before. Like everything else Rosalinda touched, there was intention and attentiveness.

She walked towards the plot where Rosalinda planted a second larger garden. She sadly thought about all of Rosalinda's work that was such a waste of energy now that she may not want to stay. There is nothing to hold Rosalinda here. Soon, maybe even today, Rosalinda will state her intention to leave. What do I have that could possibly persuade her to stay? There's nothing,

simply nothing. When Rosalinda planted this garden, she had a future tying her to this ranch. Without her, and with no one to care for it, it will surely be overrun with weeds and die.

After stocking up on supplies at Hatcher's store, Ben and Rosalinda headed back to the Curtis place with enough groceries and staples to last for several months.

Rosalinda reasoned to herself that Hattie and the children would not want for the basic necessities, even if she had no real responsibility for them. She could not understand how Earl could leave his family at such a critical time and then decided to stay away. The ranch had potential. The spread had water, and the soil was better than most in the region. Even a novice had a good chance of making it. He could have stayed; he should have stayed, and he chose to go.

Rosalinda's thoughts turned towards Hattie, as they involuntarily did with increasing frequency. As hard as she tried, Hattie was always there.

She told Ben she would leave some of her load at Hattie's and would take the majority of the load on to her own place later. However, she did not tell him she planned to re-supply Hattie's supplies each time she went back and forth. It was best if even Hattie didn't know. If her husband returned early, there would not be a lot of inventory leading him to think that Hattie had been careless with his money. To keep appearances normal, Rosalinda

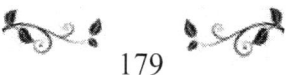

planned to charge just enough on the Curtis account for the usual paltry amount. Of course, it would not make sense to Mr. Hatcher as to why she bought so much food for herself. But she would not worry about it for now, and they would all eat well.

To her pleasant surprise she adjusted quickly to Ben's automobile machine and, even better, her horse did not fight being led by it. She also felt good that Ben did not ask any questions about her purchases, she would not know what to say if he had. Instead, their conversation meandered along other diversions.

"So," Ben said, "I heard that the town may get telephone service soon. The railroad and bank are pushing American Telephone and Telegraph to get it done. It seems to me that it wouldn't be very complicated since the poles are already up for the telegraph." He paused for a moment. "Have you ever seen a telephone work?"

"No, but I've read about them."

Ben went on, "I got to use one a couple of times back in Chicago. Amazing things, you can have a whole conversation with someone as far as the wires are strung up. I talked to someone twenty miles away as if they were sitting right next to me.

Rosalinda thought how she longed to hear her sister's voice and to tell her about their good fortune. She thought about this a little more.

"Ben, as soon as possible, we should meet in your office to make legal accommodations for my sister in case anything

happens to me. I also want to make sure that none of Hector's relatives will ever get a penny of my parents' money."

"Well, well. You've got quite the head on your shoulders. My afternoons are pretty open this week. Stop by whenever you wish. In the meantime, make a list of questions and think about what your wishes would be in the unlikely event of your demise."

Hattie was busy breast-feeding the babies when she heard the familiar sound of Ben's motorcar.

"Lourdes," Hattie called out, "Please go out and see to Mr. Bowers and tell him that I will attend to him shortly."

Lourdes was busy picking stones out of a bowl of dry navy beans, but in her excitement, she turned too quickly and spilled half of them on the floor. She immediately got down on all fours to retrieve them. "Si, Señora. I will go out and tell him." She responded while rapidly scooping them up.

By the time Lourdes finished, she had emerged from the house just in time to see the back of Ben's automobile halfway up the rise. She watched in disappointment for missing the chance to see the machine up close. It would have given her something special to talk about with her five siblings. She started back towards the house when she glimpsed a woman moving about in the barn. The shadows in the barn made it difficult for Lourdes to see who it was or what she was doing. She squinted and shaded her eyes but still couldn't make out who was there.

She was hesitant, but then her curiosity outweighed her reservations and she cautiously approached the barn. When she reached the entrance, she saw the back of a smartly dressed woman, like those she saw walking with men dressed in suits wearing white shirts with stiff collars her mother laundered and pressed at her home.

She continued moving closer for a better look. It appeared that the woman was sorting cans and boxes, most of which had been placed in burlap bags. She was so focused on her activities that she was totally unaware of Lourdes standing behind her.

"Señora?" Lourdes asked.

"Oh!" Rosalinda threw the can of hominy from her hand as if a bank robber had just demanded, "Stick 'em up!" As the can rolled by Lourdes' feet, she snatched it up. She was a bit taken aback by the way the woman reacted and was a little afraid that the woman might be angry with her.

Rosalinda, facing the equally startled child, smiled, and let out a breath of relief. Lourdes had never addressed her as "Señora" and her mind had jumped to the conclusion that it was someone else.

"Señora?" Lourdes again asked.

"What's wrong Lourdes?"

It took a moment for it to sink in, but when it did Lourdes reacted like a child finally getting the meaning of a joke. She laughed, covered her face, and then laughed again.

"Rosalinda, I did not know it was you! I thought I don't know, I thought some lady, maybe the wife of the railroad owner, was going to take Señora Curtis to the big city. I was fooled – joke on me no?"

"Well the joke was not intended, but it is good to see you laugh."

"But you are dressed like a fine lady."

"Ah, well it is a long story and I am much too busy to tell you now." She said as they walked out.

Rosalinda, reaching into her pocket, pulled out a shiny twenty-five cent piece. "Lourdes, I want you to go to Mr. Hatcher's store and buy your mother some honey for the sopapillas she's been dreaming of making, and a jar of cold cream for her poor red hands."

She nodded in understanding. "But, what about my chores? If I leave now it is too late to come back and finish. I only say this because you know my family needs my money."

"Don't worry. You will get your full wages for the day. When you are done picking up these things for your mother you are free to go home for the rest of the day."

Lourdes was so pleased she gave Rosalinda a hug.

"Go on now and tell your mother to use the cream every night and not to use so little that it does no good. Can you remember that? Oh, and you should have a few pennies left to spend on candy."

"Gracias Rosalinda," she said as her head bobbed up and down.

Rosalinda watched for a few moments as the girl scampered towards town.

She returned to the barn and found Shakespeare waiting for her. He started sniffing around the edges of her skirt and then sat down.

"Even you?" She sat on a wooden crate next to him and started stroking his head and scratching behind his ears. "Shakespeare, sometimes I think I am going crazy."

Lifting her head and looking at the house across the way, she whispered, "But I can't stop what I feel inside me no more than I can learn to stop breathing. Isn't it better to see the sunlight from the shadows then to never see the sunlight at all?" She looked back down at her friend, "Sometimes a plant, that only thrives in the full sun can survive in the shade if the rocks and earth around it reflect the light in the day and warms it a little longer when the sun goes down."

She paused for a few moments and thought, "I hope that I am like that plant. God sowed me into this earth where the sun can't touch. Then…" she turned back to look at the house, "then he placed this wonderful warm rock right next to me; a bright rock shining towards me all day and then warming me after twilight. She will not know, but maybe I can endure by just being close by. I don't know. I don't know."

"Well, enough of that," she said out loud to Shakespeare, reminding herself that there was work to do. She stood up, retrieved the can of hominy, and put it in a sack.

She worked another fifteen minutes and then gathered a group of items for the root cellar. If Earl returned she would simply tell him that it was better to have some built up stock. There would be fewer trips to town and less time away from the children.

When she was done she returned to the barn. Mindful of her new clothes, she carefully lifted a crateful of goods and brought them to the house.

They would have a nice dinner; ham steak, fried potatoes, canned sweet peas, and an enormous piece of Mrs. Hatcher's apple pandowdy. After starting the potatoes, she went about putting the rest of the items away.

Hattie opened the bedroom door and saw the back of a well-dressed woman stretching up to put a can of something on the top shelf. Quite bewildered she asked, "Excuse me, do I know you?"

With the can of corned beef still in her hands, Rosalinda turned around. For several seconds they stood face to face. Hattie was awestruck and could not move as if a magician had just cast a powerful spell on her.

She scanned every detail of Rosalinda's image: her soft black hair partially pinned up, leaving the rest to fall on her shoulders; her new clothes perfectly befitting her frame; and her face. She knew, of course, that it was Rosalinda because she recognized the sound of her movements from the other room, but

this was a shock. As she looked into Rosalinda's striking hazel eyes, she felt herself start to tremble.

Rosalinda gazed back into Hattie's face, moved nearly to tears by what she thought she saw in Hattie's eyes. Her body ached to reach out and draw her in. But the stakes were far too high to move a single inch closer. The moment became too intense, and Rosalinda compelled herself to turn her eyes away.

"Well," Rosalinda said, and then let out her breath. Her words came out choppy, but she couldn't control it, "after I get these things put away and change into my work clothes, I'd like to make us an early supper. Is that all right?"

Hattie, still locked in a half-trance uttered, "Sure, supper, early, fine." She then eased herself into the chair.

Rosalinda felt Hattie's eyes on her, and it was like the warm sun lifting her out of a life of bitter shadows. If only she could stop the world from turning right here and now. Then Rosalinda's thoughts snapped her back to the harsh reality. No place on earth would allow her to share what she so desperately wanted to share with Hattie. Confused and ashamed she turned away to avoid Hattie's probing eyes and resumed putting the butter beans on the shelf. She would stick to her compromise, her borrowed piece of happiness she mapped out in her mind just a short while ago. It was the only way.

Hattie, watching her, noticed how Rosalinda's strong shoulders tapered perfectly down to her splendidly-curved waist. She wondered how it would feel to gently lay her hand upon

Rosalinda's cheek. She closed her eyes and shook her head to clear the thought.

"No, not fine!" Hattie blurted.

Rosalinda turned back around, "All right then, but supper will be much later than normal, I…"

Hattie put up her hand like an impatient school girl demanding the teacher's attention. In a sharp tone, she said, "That's not what I mean!"

Rosalinda pulled out a chair, sat down, and patiently waited for Hattie to speak her mind.

Hattie took an extra breath to gather her thoughts. "The last time I saw you, you looked like God had personally told you that the sun would never shine again, ever. I thought it was because you were afraid for your sister. But after you knew she was safe and there was a plan to reach her, it didn't seem to make a difference. If it weren't for Shakespeare here, I'd have guessed you would not have returned at all."

Hattie's voice was rising with frustration. "In fact,…"

She stopped dead in her tracks. It was as if she had been running full force and was skidding on loose gravel to the edge of a cliff. She didn't dare go further.

Oh, how she wanted to say, "You never even looked my way since last night." But, thank God, she caught herself in midair.

And now, struggling to say anything at all, she looked down at her lap. As the seconds passed she could tell her face was flushed red and she hated the betrayal of it.

187

"In fact?" Rosalinda asked softly. Still no response, but she noticed tears gathering in the corners of Hattie's eyes.

"I'm sorry, I shouldn't have barked at you," Hattie said while trying to hide an escaping tear. "I've heard of women getting all emotional after delivering a baby; I never thought it would happen to me. I was stronger than that you know. I wasn't one of them; those frail only-good-for-lookin'-at women." She looked up and feigned a chuckle, "Hah, I guess having two babies was past my limit. Sorry."

Of course, there was some truth in her words, but it felt like a lie. It felt like the biggest lie she had ever told. And it was.

"Sure, I understand. You're right. A lot of new mothers feel like they're under a dark cloud for weeks on end. It takes a while you know – to adjust to the big changes in your life."

Hattie was thinking, "Oh you don't know how much! You wouldn't want to know how much."

"Listen," Rosalinda continued, "Why don't you lay down until supper is ready or until the children wake up? You still need your rest."

Hattie wiped away another tear and nodded in compliance. Then, she stood up and quickly glanced about the room at the stacks of items and food. She would ask Rosalinda about them later.

She softly closed the door behind her and then walked over to check on the babies. "How beautiful they are. What's wrong with Earl? How could he hurry himself away from his part of

God's miracles? Maybe it's best he's not here. Oh, I don't know."

Careful not to wake them, she bent down and smelled the top of Clayton's head and then Martha's. She slowly pulled in their scents and immediately felt a shift in her emotions. There were no questions here, no doubts, no boundaries, and no conditions to this love. She gently stroked the silky-fine hair on each of them and then curled up on the bed.

Her thoughts moved once again to Rosalinda as she listened to the muffled noises as she moved about in the other room. Then her thoughts meandered to Earl. She felt betrayed and abandoned by Earl – he had a duty, an obligation that was conveniently set aside for his own pursuits. There were signs; weren't there? He hadn't said anything, but she knew it would only be a matter of time before he would leave.

She stared at the ceiling and began recalling their relationship. He had quite unexpectantly showed up and proposed marriage pressuring her much like that tonic-selling Dr. Goodhealer. Earl, and his good looks mesmerized her and he could have sold her a drink of water if she were drowning in the middle of the Rio Grande.

She never thought much about how that day unfolded, but now it seemed important. She recalled that Earl was anxious to marry before leaving town even though she argued that her parent's minister would be happy to perform a quick ceremony. And why was he so surly after they left her parent's home when he was almost giddy on the train? Something had disappointed him; was it her?

Hattie thought about that for a minute. She remembered that when she was eleven she overheard her mother and Cassie talking about "men's special appetites." The two of them continued to talk in hushed tones, sometimes giggling, but abruptly stopped when her father appeared from his study. At the time none of it made sense, but it certainly did now. "No, that can't be it," she thought, "On our wedding night I even asked Earl what I could do to please him, but he looked at me like I tried to feed him a mud pie. He didn't seem to enjoy it at all. When we did, it was like he was just releasing some unpleasant built-up pressure, like something he had to do, like discharging the contents of an angry, ugly boil."

Hattie shuddered at her own thoughts. Even though they shared their bed as man and wife, the way he touched her made her feel used and dirty.

Hindsight has such clarity. How was it that she so easily believed Earl when he said, "The last of the west is waiting for us. History was being written and it needed two more names; Earl and Hattie!"

She softly groaned, "Stupid, stupid, stupid," then turned over and watched Rosalinda's shadow flit back and forth under the door.

Rosalinda changed into her new work clothes and carefully folded her dress clothes into the used brown paper wrapping. Having no storage area of her own was now posing to be problematic. She made yet another mental note to bring over the old leather case her mother had held on to. It was once used for her father's pharmaceutical samples. It was smaller than a steamer trunk, but a little larger than a suitcase. It would fit nicely under the cot.

"Under the cot?" she thought. "This is getting complicated."

Her thoughts turned back to preparing dinner but based on Hattie's peculiar mood wasn't sure if she'd be up to it.

Rosalinda knocked softly on the door, "Hattie?" Rosalinda waited, "Hattie can I come in?" Hattie opened the door then quickly sat down on the chair she positioned next to the sleeping babies. To her amazement, Hattie was now smiling and motioned to Rosalinda to take a look. Rosalinda approached as Hattie continued to wave her closer and then pointed. Baby Clayton had somehow maneuvered himself in such a way that he was now sucking on Martha Rose's thumb.

Hattie whispered, "Isn't that a hoot?"

Rosalinda leaned slightly over Hattie to get a better look. Little Clayton was suckling and appeared just as happy with sister's thumb as though it was his own. She had a passing thought that he likely got this trait from his father. But, the scene was just too cute, and thoughts of Earl quickly dissipated.

"Don't forget to write to you folks about this."

All of Hattie's worries of a few minutes ago melted away. Her children were safe and healthy, she was nearly well, and Rosalinda was smiling and enjoying this special moment with her.

They both happily watched for a few more moments and then Rosalinda straightened up and put her hands on her hips to stretch out her tired back.

In a half whisper she said, "Supper will be ready soon." Then, as she turned, she reached out and gave Hattie a little pat on her shoulder.

"Is there anything I can do to help?"

"No, no. You just stay here and enjoy. I'll let you know when it's ready."

Hattie continued enjoying her babies but, more so, savored the recollection of the last few minutes. When Rosalinda leaned over her to get a closer view, she had gently leaned against her and her intoxicating scent lingered, like smelling the fragrance of a patch of lilacs long after passing through it. Perhaps it clings to you and you can carry it for a while. Hattie tried to pick out the scents: soap, salt, earth, and something undefinable, alluring, and mind-altering. It had made her blood rush and her face feel hot. She could bury herself in it, get lost in her scent forever, and die happy – if she could, only if she could.

Chapter Fifteen – Willy Quinn's Place

The next day Rosalinda packed up the food on the burro to be stored at her ranch. She tied the lead to her horse and picked her way down the dry washes and hills. Every so often she caught herself closing her eyes to remember the brief moment when she leaned over Hattie. Then she shook her head to keep the horse on track. He was not used to the route and had to be skillfully guided along.

When they came in view of the old house she began to think about ways to improve the place; to make a fresh start. The shed needed to be torn down; maybe the house too.

She mulled this over for a bit, but then remembered overhearing a conversation four months ago between the old timers sitting on the bench in front of Mr. Hatcher's store; it was about Willy Quinn.

"Yeah," old Earnest said to Grover, "It doesn't surprise me. I can't blame Willy for wanting to go to Tulsa to work in his brother's hardware store. His spread's too small to support a herd big enough to turn a profit. He's hoping for a buyer, but no one wants to make the same mistake he did."

Earnest was right about Willy's place; no profit-minded person would ever consider it. He spent nearly all his money to

drill a good well and even got a water tank and a Halladay Standard Windmill setting him back one hundred and thirty dollars. But there just wasn't enough good grazing land to make a go of it. The only good soil was located near the house and could be cultivated for a decent garden, but that was it.

But Willy's place had one feature that she would gladly pay a king's ransom; it bordered the Curtis ranch. It would take thirty minutes to travel from house to house by wagon; but by horse, ten minutes, or maybe five if it was an emergency.

She was glad she remembered this and felt optimistic as she put away her store of items and tended to the animals. When she was done she located her father's empty leather case and strapped it to her burro.

She mounted her horse and then gave her property a puzzled look. What would she do with it?

A few hours later she rode over to Willy's place. He was a tall, thin man in his early thirties who looked ten years older than he should. He had just descended from greasing the gears housed in a box behind the windmill blades when he saw Rosalinda approaching. He waved then called out towards the open door of the house, "Claire, Claire honey, Rosalinda's come for a visit."

Claire emerged from the house shading her eyes from the sun, "Well, I'll be," she said waving to her with a broad, inviting smile. Rosalinda noticed that she also had aged greatly over the past three years. "Come on in, I've got a fresh pot of coffee brewin'."

Willy and Claire were actually the second set of owners. The first owners came to New Mexico hoping the climate would help their nine-year-old son recover from tuberculosis. He seemed to improve for several months, but he eventually relapsed and died. The parents couldn't stand the loss and the memories tied to the place and so retreated with their sorrows to the mother's hometown back in Missouri.

They had left behind a three-bedroom house with a loft, parlor, and a spacious living room. And, the bank was more than pleased to mortgage the place for the balance. Since the balance was so low, when Willy put in the windmill he was easily approved for a loan to install indoor plumbing. The house was a bargain, but not for someone who needed to generate an income off the land. Unfortunately, Willy's inexperience took the better of him.

"I'm going to miss this house," Claire said to Rosalinda as she handed her and Willy a cup of coffee. "But Lord, I won't miss worrying about where the money is going to come from."

He took a sip and said, "As soon as we can sell this place we'll be on our way to Tulsa. Problem is, everyone around these parts want bigger parcels. We'll just have to keep praying."

Rosalinda piped in, "That's why I'm here!" she beamed.

"I didn't know you were devout, but if you want to pray with us I guess that would be fine," Claire said awkwardly, looking to Willy for concurrence.

"No, no," Rosalinda laughed, "I'm here to buy the property."

They still looked puzzled.

"I have money. I'm your buyer!"

She took a route that was about the way a crow would fly except for a small hill blocking the line of sight between the Quinn and the Curtis places. She made her way around the hill and stopped to look down at the Curtis place. She gave the horse a pat while she thought about what to do with her other property.

This new home would be much more practical for her and Cecelia. And it was one of the better-built homes in the area but understated enough to suit her tastes. Best of all, those learning of her new standing would expect her to find a better home, so no one would question her motivation to buy Willy's place.

She reflected on how drab and depressing the old place was with its tired windows, broken fence, and flaking walls. Her mother's attempts to convince Hector to apply a fresh coat of white-wash were ignored. One would have better luck asking the cat to do the laundry. So, Rosalina or her mother did all the repairs or maintenance. They studied each problem and then tried to figure it out. If they couldn't figure it out they asked Mr. Hatcher for advice. Sometimes, if Hector was off to one of his cock fights, Mr. Hatcher secretly came over to do the repairs.

But repairs were just that; repairs. The house was as ugly as old stained underwear; it was useful, nothing else.

Perhaps this was why her mother meticulously gathered wildflower seeds. When the time was just right, she sowed them all around the property so there would be something to look forward to in the spring. Rosalinda decided she would gather seeds from her mother's wild flowers and do the same around her new home.

Besides the wildflowers, there was nothing else there to miss. There were a few friendly neighbors, so she could easily ride over for a visit. These families were poor with little to no prospects of improving their plight. Their meager plots of mostly rented land could not sustain more than a goat and a few chickens. By comparison to her neighbors, her old ranch was grand.

"That's it!" she blurted, causing her horse to throw up his head. "I'll let the neighbors use the land." She gave him a couple of gentle kicks and started a slow canter towards Hattie's.

Her mind was bursting with possibilities. Why not spread some of her good fortune? Lourdes' family, who bordered on the east, could use the front of the property and the house to expand their laundry business. The Allesandro family, who bordered on the west, could use the backfield for a cow, and maybe a few goats.

She would assign to Mateo, the Allesandros' ten-year-old son, the old vegetable garden. He had frequently visited her when she tended to her garden; he'd love it.

Rosalinda smiled as she recalled him telling her, "Someday I will have a big farm and grow pole beans, squash, and chilies of every color."

She remembered telling him, "That's very good Mateo. I will be sure to only buy my chilies from you." She knew that it would only be a couple of years before he was hired out to local farmers. Then it wouldn't be much longer before he left his family for the rest of his life to follow the ripening crops. Rosalinda figured that whatever the garden produced for Mr. Hatcher, he could at least buy a solid pair of shoes

Her thoughts jumped forward as she imagined that in a couple of seasons he could save enough to purchase a decent travel kit for when he eventually joined the invisible throngs of migrant workers. He could buy a good sleeping blanket, a sturdy oil-cloth for rain protection, a small iron frying pan, a large jackknife, a pruning knife, utensils, and soap.

She sighed as she contemplated his bleak future. He was a good boy. And, with a little bit of luck, he would grow up to be a man who always helped his family before spending one penny on a cockfight. If she could teach him how to plan, cultivate, and sell crops for profit; he would gain confidence and perhaps avoid becoming a migrant worker. She would give him most of the proceeds for his efforts. She would keep the remaining money in reserve for him. She wasn't sure what it would be for, but it seemed like a good idea.

She furrowed her brow as she thought about how to broach these ideas with her neighbors; it would not work if they thought it was for charity. The Lord knows they could use a healthy dose of charity, but it must not come off that way.

By the time she opened the barn door, Rosalinda came up with a possible solution. In exchange, Lourdes mother could do laundry for her, and Cecelia and Mateo's father could provide the labor to put the old house into a presentable condition, including a new coat of whitewash. The clean appearance would, in turn, help the laundry business. After all, how could the clothes be clean if they are laundered in a dirty house? She was quite proud of her ideas!

She put her horse and burro in their stalls and portioned off a square of alfalfa for each. She picked up her father's leather case, gave them a quick pat on their heads, and headed towards the house.

As she got closer, she smelled frying onions and hot biscuits. The door pushed open as Shakespeare darted out to greet her.

"There you are. I was hoping you wouldn't be too late."

"Am I late? I, I didn't know I was supposed to be…"

"Oh, never mind. I'm just giving you a hard time. Supper is just about ready. I know it's a little early. Why don't you go splash some water on your face, and I'll finish up?"

Rosalinda stood motionless.

"Go on now. Oh, and don't let Shakespeare fool you into feeding him; he ate already." She then disappeared back into the house.

Chapter Sixteen – Like a Carousel

Earl, sitting on a large sandstone rock, stared into the fire throwing pebbles one by one into the flames. He was mad at himself, and as each rock hit the burning wood, it created short bursts of popping sparks.

The men seated around the fire watched Earl clench his jaw tighter and tighter with each deliberate throw. They remained silent, glancing at Earl, and then each other until the last aim caused a cascade of flying embers onto Pete's bedroll.

"Hey, you little pecker!" Pete screamed. "Whatever you've got stuck up your ass, take it away from here or I'll shove it in higher with my right foot!"

Earl had to relieve himself anyway, so he simply got up and walked away. He then hoisted himself on the seat of the wagon a few yards away. He saw that the men were talking, and from their glances, probably about him, but he didn't care.

"Twins," he said, in a slow sarcastic tone. "She went and had twins. Ain't that just sittin' pretty as can be. Dang, one step forward, two steps back; make that ten steps back. Shit."

Sitting back, he looked at the stars and shook his head as if questioning the callous intentions of his maker. Pulling out a pouch of tobacco and papers from his shirt pocket, he carefully filled and rolled a cigarette and calmed down. Maybe it was the routine of filling the paper with tobacco that helped him relax, or maybe he was temporarily done fighting with himself and was now content to lament.

He lit up, took a long drag, held it, and then blew it out as if he was extinguishing a stubborn candle. The next drag was easy, and his mind wandered back to his ranch-hand days in northern Texas and the last time he saw Amanda.

"Yeah," he thought. That was a disaster too." But at least her father had the brains to hand him a hundred dollars just to stay away. She was pretty, but not too pretty to pass up a hundred dollars. Now he was stuck with a wife and two bawling, shit-making machines.

He hawked back a lump of mucous and spit at an invisible target. His anger began to return as he thought about Hattie's father. The old bastard had to be rich, hell he had a thriving business. He should have backed them for two or three years 'till the ranch started to turn a real profit. And the house; he should have forked over enough to build a decent one. A three bedroom would have been nice, hell even a two bedroom. But no, not even a single plank of lumber!

He pondered this and then a thought seared into his brain like a sizzling branding iron. Hattie must have told her father they didn't need his charity! He jumped up. "That little bitch!" he blurted out, momentarily catching the men's attention. He was oblivious to them and morbidly enjoyed his revelation. Hattie was the true cause of his failed life.

Rosalinda started to get up to clear the dishes.

"Oh no you don't, you just stay put. This time I'm taking care of you. Besides, it feels good to do for others for a change." She picked up the dishes placing them in the galvanized tub. "Would you like some coffee or some of that tea that magically appeared behind the cornmeal? The water is already hot."

"Tea would be fine. Would you sit and have a cup with me?"

"Of course, I will. It'll be ready in a couple of minutes."

When the tea finished steeping Hattie settled back down at the table.

Rosalinda took a sip and looked up. "I was thinking I should be staying at my own place now that you're feeling better and, well, my circumstances have changed."

Hattie looked crestfallen. She knew this would happen eventually, even knew the change made sense, but she didn't like it.

"But," Rosalinda went on, "I still intend to help you, but not because I'm paid to do it. And I'd like to still work in the vegetable garden, as Earl agreed I could."

Hattie nodded her understanding. Her demeanor improved slightly but knew that she would miss being able to simply talk to her whenever she wanted. She also knew that Rosalinda would

soon be so busy at her old home she would see her less and less. Her old friends and neighbors would want her back; who wouldn't?

"But why do you still want to work the garden? You certainly don't need the paltry amount of money the crops would likely bring."

Rosalinda had anticipated her question. "Actually, I have three reasons. First, you still need a little more instruction on growing vegetables to their full potential. Second, Mr. Hatcher says that the town is growing so fast that he won't be able to keep up with the demand for produce. And third, there is this boy; his name is Mateo that I may bring along every now and then to teach him as well."

Rosalinda paused to make sure Hattie was following along, then asked, "That is" she paused again, "if you want me to teach you. Also, if it's all right with you, I'd like Earl to think that you did the work and I just showed you some of the basics; which would not be a lie. Anyway, Mr. Hatcher would be happy to pay you directly, so that you will have your own money."

Hattie didn't know quite what to say. At least Rosalinda wasn't planning to disappear completely; at least not until the garden had been harvested. At least she could still see her a couple of times a week.

"Yes," Hattie quietly responded, "I like all of what you said." But she still had a shade of sadness in her voice.

They sat quietly as Rosalinda watched Hattie take several more sips and tried to calculate how she would react to the next part of her plan.

"I guess I should be getting to those dishes; the water is probably getting cold."

Rosalinda motioned her to stop. "Wait, please, I need to tell you something else."

Hattie, anticipating something dreadful, sat back down.

"Willy and Claire Quinn are moving back to Tulsa in a couple of days." Hattie had no idea where this was going. Why was she telling her this?

"And," Rosalinda paused and took another sip.

"And?" Hattie questioned.

"And, I will be your new neighbor. I bought the house today."

Hattie beamed like a child getting exactly what she wanted for her birthday.

"That's wonderful! Th… that's great!" Hattie was ecstatic! She placed both her hands on top of her head as if she just stopped an invisible hat from blowing off her head. "That's wonderful," she repeated.

Rosalinda stood up to join in her happiness and laughed.

Hattie twirled about and caught Rosalinda up like a square dancer about to do an Allemande left when they wrapped each other up in one another's arms. Like a top they spun around

quickly and then...and then, they began to slow down. They continued holding on to each other and as the seconds passed they increasingly sensed the intense longing of the other...in each breath...in each breath they heard, smelled, and now felt their breath on each other's necks.

Like a carousel making its final round, they too were nearly at a stop.

Rosalinda let go just enough to gaze into Hattie's eyes. They each seemed to be asking the same questions – can this be real? Can I be so fortunate that you came into my life; to make me feel this way? Are you as scared as I am; because I'm very, very scared? Is it possible to go on?"

Suddenly there was thunderous knocking at the door. Rosalinda and Hattie split apart as violent as a lightning bolt splitting a tree right down the middle. They both felt like they had just been lassoed off a speeding horse.

The door pounded again, and a familiar voice called out, "Rosalinda, Rosalinda, this is..."

Rosalinda unlatched the door. It was Silas, but he wasn't in his deputy uniform. "Silas, what's the matter? What's going on? Come in."

"Sorry to bother you, and you too Mrs. Curtis."

The words "Mrs. Curtis" stung. Rosalinda winced as he said them but luckily, he didn't see her reaction. Shakespeare appeared from behind Silas and sat down beside him.

"No wonder Shakespeare didn't bark; he knows you too well."

He continued, "Dr. Pierce needs your help right away. Seems your lawyer accidently drove his automobile into a ravine and is in pretty bad shape."

"Oh my!" Hattie gasped.

"Silas, you go on ahead and tell Dr. Pierce I'll be there as soon as possible. I'll grab a few things and ride in. At least there are a few more hours of daylight."

"All right then, I'll let him know," he said and then got on his horse and trotted towards town."

Rosalinda turned to Hattie, "I'm sorry, I really have to go. Hopefully I'll be back tomorrow, but it could be a couple of days."

"I understand. Please tell Ben that I'll be praying for his speedy recovery."

She didn't know how long she would be needed as she gathered up nearly all her clothes and a few essentials. Even though she told Hattie she hoped to be back the next day, she knew if Dr. Pierce sent Silas out to get her, it must be serious.

Hattie followed her out on the porch and touched her on the elbow. "Now don't be in such a hurry that you end up falling off Zuzu."

"I'll be careful." Rosalinda caught Hattie's hand, gave it a quick squeeze, and headed off.

Chapter Seventeen – The Poem

When Rosalinda reached Dr. Pierce's place it was too quiet. A man with broken limbs or large wounds would be moaning, screaming, or at least cursing.

She dropped her things on a chair in the waiting area and rushed into the surgery room. Dr. Pierce had just given Ben an injection and was sitting on a stool.

Ben, or at least some poor creature who was supposed to be Ben, was laying on his back with his head propped on a pillow. She noticed that his face, especially his mouth and cheeks were so badly abraded, he almost looked like a circus clown.

She stepped closer and could hear his faint moans. He seemed to be trying to speak.

"Ben, don't try to speak, you need to save your energy," she said as she gently touched the top of his head.

She looked down the length of his body trying to get a quick sense of the damage, although she knew Dr. Pierce had certainly made a full assessment. Why was Ben still in his suit coat? She saw blood seeping through both elbows and was certain there would be lacerations under his torn shirt and vest. She also saw blotches of red soaking through the vest.

When Dr. Pierce entered the room, she was relieved.

"I'll cut these clothes away for you; or would you rather I get the bandages and sutures ready?" Rosalinda impatiently waited for instructions, but Dr. Pierce did not reply for several seconds.

Looking down at the hypodermic needle, he said "the morphine will take care of the pain, the rest is up for God to decide."

"What? That's it?" Rosalinda shook her head in disbelief. "I've seen you save beat-up and shot-up drunks who were in a lot worse shape than Ben. I don't understand; it doesn't look like you've even examined him to see how deep his wounds are; this, this just doesn't make any sense at all." Her voice began to rise as she pleaded, "Why won't you help him?"

"Now don't get all high and mighty on me!" he shot back. There was another moment of silence as he gained his composure. "After Silas took off to get you, I got the rest of the story." He took out his pipe and lit it.

He turned to Rosalinda, "You haven't taken a really good look at him. Go on, look. Look at his face; there are a few cuts, but the rest is lipstick; lipstick smeared on him by a few strong men while half a dozen pillars of the community watched and cheered. After they found the poems, it only took a few minutes before word got out. The next thing you know the nearest saloon emptied out, and well, the hunt was on."

"Wait. What poems? What on earth would poems even remotely have to do with this! This sounds more insane by the minute." Looking through the sheer curtains, she saw that a group was gathered out front. The ladies were frowning and shaking their heads; while the young men, apparently amused with the situation, were whispering, and laughing.

She turned towards Ben, trying to fightback her tears. The morphine had slowed Ben's breathing and he no longer tried to communicate.

She turned back around, "Why am I here if you're going to just let him die?"

"Like I said, Silas had already left." Dr. Pierce pointed the tip of his pipe towards the kitchen and Rosalinda reluctantly followed.

He leaned back against the counter and motioned for Rosalinda to take a seat.

"Rosalinda, there are just some things, evil things, in this world that people hardly talk about, even in private. Now I know your stepfather was a despicable man and those he chose to run with weren't much better. But now Mr. Bowers, well he's a disgrace to all humanity. Even Hector had a better chance to get into heaven."

Rosalinda squeezed her eyes shut as she thought, what could be worse than a father lusting after his own daughter?

"What happened?" Rosalinda asked.

"Do you recollect Wayne, the young office clerk, who worked upstairs with Mr. Bowers and the other businessmen? Anyway, he did typing and such for them and apparently Mr. Bowers left some work for him on his desk. When Wayne

went to pick up the pile of papers to bring back to his typewriter, he noticed something sticking out from under the blotter. I guess his curiosity got the better of him and he pulled it out to see what was hiding there. He then read the lot of it."

Dr. Pierce's pipe went out, but this time he didn't try to re-light it. He stared into the tobacco bowl just to focus on something. "It turns out they were love poems. Love poems to a man. I always thought he was a bit of a fancy dresser, but love poems to a man?"

Rosalinda's immediate impulse was to run. She felt her face burning with fear, shame, guilt, and humiliation. She knew she had to stay and hear the rest of what Dr. Pierce would say. She instinctively knew that every derogatory word directed at Ben would, if the truth be known, apply equally to her. An abhorred category of humankind existed, but until this moment she never looked into that internal mirror acknowledging membership. She didn't have a word for it, but she knew.

Dr. Pierce continued talking, and did not notice that Rosalinda's face was as still as a corpse. She couldn't move from the sheer terror of her predicament. She was like a rabbit holding still, praying that the predator wouldn't notice.

"Well Wayne did the right thing and showed what he had found to his boss Dan Edwards. You know him?"

Rosalinda nodded and let him continue.

"Then Dan informed the rest of the men on the second floor who in turn informed the rest of the men in the building. The bank manager went on over to report the matter to Silas, so he

could get a warrant started. Meanwhile a group of citizens went out after Mr. Bowers to make Silas's job easier."

Rosalinda forced herself to engage in the conversation, but was sickened by her silent rage and shame, "So what did Silas do?" She said, all the while thinking of Ben who lay dying in the next room.

"Despite Silas' dumb looks, he's got a pretty good head. He told Dan that a warrant wasn't necessary if someone eventually reported a possible accident, and maybe jotted down the whereabouts.

About an hour or so later, the Timken sisters happened across the scene and reported the accident. So, Silas and Billy headed out with a wagon. You see, by that time everyone who may have been present when it happened was long gone – back to the saloons or home.

The old Timken sisters just came along and noticed a car turned over in a ditch on their way back from Santa Rosa. It was too steep to get a good look, so they made a beeline into town. So, it was just an accident, at least that's what Billy told me when he dropped Ben off. That's when I sent Silas on after you. A few minutes later Dan came over and filled me in on the real details."

He paused for a moment, "No one has figured out the man in the poem. Dan showed one of them to me. Part of it said something like, 'When I see you dance, my heart dances with you." And the rest was just plain repulsive. "Would you like some lemonade?"

Inside her head she was screaming, "Father Palo! Oh Lord will he be next?" But she knew she couldn't do or say anything right now that seemed the least bit unusual. Her mind was spinning. It is only a matter of time before people begin to piece together who Ben had spent his time with. Once again, she fought down the urge to run.

"I'll take just half a glass. This accident will probably put my mother's estate in a mess, so I need to see Mr. Edwards right away."

He reached into the cooler and poured her half a glass. "You're right. You best take care of business."

They heard the front door open and Dr. Pierce found Mrs. Langley helping her moaning husband to sit down. "He's gone and dislocated his shoulder again," she explained.

While Dr. Pierce started to work on him Rosalinda sneaked into see Ben for the last time. His eyes were open, and he watched her as she came to his side.

She bent down close to his ear, "I'm so sorry Ben, oh so, so sorry. I will warn Father Palo. Don't worry; I'll make sure he is safe." She fought back the tears. "I've got to go now before it's too late."

His face was the color of white clay and she knew it wouldn't be much longer before he passed. His lips began to move, and Rosalinda put her ear near his mouth. His words were barely discernible, but she understood, "Thank you. Go now." He didn't inhale, he was gone.

She found the front door locked when she got to the church. To her knowledge it had never been locked. Father Navarro and his successor, Father Palo, believed that anyone needing God, or refuge from the heat or cold should find this house of God welcoming. Now it was inaccessible. Maybe God was inaccessible today as well.

She hurried to the side door and found it locked as well. The breeze picked up and was blowing leaves around as if an invisible person was busy sweeping. She quickly walked around the outbuildings. One was a small shop for keeping tools and maintenance equipment, and another shed to store extra chairs and odd pieces of furniture; but no one was around. She scanned the grounds and then noticed a narrow foot path leading down to a dry stream bed. She followed it for several minutes and stopped when she heard a man sobbing; it was coming from behind a large boulder.

As she came closer she called out, "Father Palo is that you? It's Rosalinda. I desperately need to talk with you." There was no answer although the sobbing had stopped. She drew closer.

"I can't help you Rosalinda, not now. Please not now."

"I'm not here for you to help me, I'm here to help you," she exclaimed as she rounded the boulder.

215

He was laying on the ground, his knees pulled up tight into his chest, his hands over his head as if to shield himself from the falling sky. He made himself as small as a man could physically make himself. She knelt next to him and wrapped her arms around him.

"I know you are the man in the poems and we've got to get you out of here before anyone else figures it out. We've got to go now."

He looked up. "Ben, Ben, do you know anything? Where is he; at Dr. Pierce's? Oh God, tell me he's not dead."

Rosalinda knew that each second they lingered was another second closer to Father Palo's reckoning with the town's good citizens. She hated to do it, but she lied. "I was with Ben when he passed, and he made me promise to help you to safety. Do you understand? Ben wanted you safe."

He started bawling like a baby. And then she heard the whistle of the train coming into the station.

"Father," she tried to rouse him, "Father!" she said with a stern voice.

He sobbed on, "I'm not fit to be a Father, an Altar boy, or anything else. I've failed everyone, including God, by just being alive."

"Stand up," she demanded but he would not move. "Stand up. You must be on that train before it pulls out. We only have half an hour and you've got to gather your things." He continued to whimper.

Rosalinda could not wait a second longer. He was in peril and could not see beyond his grief. Taking a breath for courage, she grabbed a large handful of his hair, yanked it back and slapped him hard across his face. She pulled him up to his feet by the front of his shirt. Then she held him up against the boulder and wouldn't let him budge.

"You listen to me. For the next half hour, you're going to straighten up and pretend that everything is normal. If someone gets close to us, you will pretend to sneeze and cough like you've got the worst allergies since Noah realized he was allergic to fur. At least that'll explain your puffy eyes and red nose."

"But I don't have anywhere to go. I only know church people. Will you take care of Ben's arrangements?"

She felt he was beginning to understand the situation and loosened her grip. He slid several inches down the side of the boulder before he stood on his own feet.

"Yes, I'll see to it that he has a decent final resting place. And we'll figure where you go from here before we buy the ticket."

Back at the church she instructed him to grab only what fit into one bag. She would come back and meet him in a few minutes. She stayed just long enough to watch him start packing and then hurried to the bank to make a withdrawal and then to the mercantile store. Fortunately, there was no line at the bank and only a few customers milling about the store. Father Palo was

about her size, so no one would notice if she bought work trousers and three men's shirts; one shirt a little dressier than the others. She also purchased two plain-brown travelling bags.

When Rosalinda returned to the church, she was relieved to see he was ready to go.

"Here," she handed him one bag, "put your things in here and I'll put the rest in the other bag."

"What are those packages?" he asked as he filled his bag.

"Trousers and shirts. I don't think you will find a church willing to take you on after today, so you better change your clothing after you have travelled at least a few towns away. Hurry, we don't have much time."

To be on the safe side they stayed off the main street, walking behind the shops until they reached the back of the station. Stepping onto the platform they saw a few passengers boarding and the last few pallets of ice blocks coming off the end cars. They stood close to the building and to the side of a rain barrel.

"I want you to go to Saint Louis."

He looked puzzled, but she continued. "I want you to go to Saint Louis and find those theater people you talked about. You take any job you can with them; cleaning, selling tickets, ushering, anything. Eventually you could show them that you can dance."

"What if they won't hire me?"

"Then find out where they room and board and stay there until you hear of an opening. You can find some other kind of work, and you need to be able to know when they need help. So, I'm going in to get you a ticket to Saint Louis. Do you understand?"

He nodded, and she went inside. She was relieved to find that the man at the ticket counter wasn't from around here and the passengers had already cleared the area. He completed the transaction without even looking up and told her to hurry and get on board.

She found Father Palo slowly making his way towards the passenger car, so the conductor could see that there was one more rider.

"Here," she handed him his ticket and an envelope. "This will get you by for several months as long as you don't do anything extravagant."

"Oh no, I couldn't."

"You will, and you must!" Rosalinda sternly replied.

With the train's big brass bell ringing, the conductor motioned him to board. He turned back to Rosalinda and quickly held her tight against his chest.

"Thank you. Thank you for everything."

"Let me know where you are as soon as possible, but don't put your real name on the return address."

He looked around to be sure he was out of ear shot, "Whose name should I use?" he said as he stepped up into the train.

Rosalinda thought for a second, "Well you're going to Saint Louis, how about Sam Lewis with a 'W'?

"Yes, Sam Lewis it is," he said, then went to find a seat.

Rosalinda stayed hidden as she watched the train pull away and took the back way from the station.

Back at the bank building she left a note for Dan Edwards letting him know she would contact him soon to discuss her estate. At least if Dr. Pierce ran into Dan, her story would match.

She made her way to Dr. Pierce's office from the bank. The group who gathered earlier were gone now. The show they hoped to see never materialized. What did they think they would see anyway? Was Satan going to spring up from hell and haul away Ben's battered body?

She walked by the same window and saw that a sheet now covered his body. She hated it but had to put on a false front once again.

When she got to the porch, Dr. Pierce was in a rocking chair smoking his pipe as though nothing unusual happened today.

"Ah, Rosalinda, I didn't expect to see you back here today. Come and sit a spell."

She sat down on the vacant rocker next to his. "I forgot that I left my things in the parlor. So, how's Mr. Langley? I personally never had a dislocation, it sure looked like it hurt a great deal."

"Oh, he's fine except Mrs. Langley is not likely to let him off the hook for hurting himself. Probably be more painful than the actual injury."

"I suppose you are right." Rosalinda said. She casually rocked back and forth a few times and lightly batted away a bothersome fly.

"So, what's going to happen now with Mr. Bowers' remains?"

"Well Silas said he'd wire Mr. Bowers' brother in California. If he doesn't respond by tomorrow night, the town will throw him in a hole in the west cemetery. He'll be lucky if he gets a wooden plank with his name on it. Why do you ask?"

"You might think I'm crazy, but he did a heck of a lot of digging and research with people back east to secure my estate, and he went out on a limb trying to find my sister. I, well I feel, that despite all this unpleasantness, my conscience would rest a lot easier if he had a halfway decent final resting place, possibly in the next county. If his brother doesn't respond will you please ask the undertaker to contact me? I'll be at my mother's place tonight and tomorrow."

"Well, I know how important it is to have a clear conscious. Sure, I'll let him know."

She lingered just long enough to not raise any suspicion, gathered up her things, and then said goodnight.

She thought about going back to see Hattie, to let her know everything that had happened. She needed some time to think, to take a breath, to cry. But even that would have to wait just a little longer.

Chapter Eighteen – Credible Reasons

As she drew closer to her mother's small ranch, the severity of her own situation haunted her. "Disgrace to humanity," that's what Dr. Pierce called it. Oh God, he just let him die. He'd let me die too.

She put Zuzu in the barn, giving him an extra portion of oats. She then brought her things into the house. How ironic, she thought, that this house, with all its terrible memories, was now her place of refuge.

She sat at the table wishing there was a bottle of anything to dull her senses. Reality, ugly reality, called her name. If anyone knew who she really was, they would find a way to be rid of her. When that time came it wouldn't matter who or how many of them she loved, cared for, or was there for, in their direst needs. It wouldn't matter how much they loved her mother or her sister – they would turn on her. She would be as welcome as a rabid dog, and everyone knew what happened to rabid dogs.

Putting her head down on her folded arms, she sobbed. She sobbed for the pain, suffering, and shame that Ben endured this day. She sobbed for the plight, fear, and grief that Father Palo must bear alone. She sobbed as she had watched Dr. Pierce let her friend die and she had to pretend, pretend, pretend!

Suddenly, she stopped sobbing as a nightmarish thought exploded in her mind, "Hattie would also be a target if the gossip turned towards us. The children would be damaged forever." She sat motionless, then bringing her hands to her mouth she whispered, "Oh God."

She paced from room to room all evening. Her mind buzzed about like a fly trapped in a room, bouncing off one wall only to crash head on into another. After a while Rosalinda went outside and paced from the barn to the house and back to the barn again under the moonlit sky. Every few minutes she started to cry, but defiantly fought back her tears. She would not, could not, let anything happen to Hattie and the children. How could she protect them?

After hours of thinking, the only thing she figured out was that she should not take any rash actions. If she left now after today's events it would only raise questions and turn the attention in Hattie's direction. Leaving things as they were only invited disaster. The town's people relish the gossip, their imaginations running in every direction. They would be looking for anything to talk about. Rosalinda knew this event would just be a stepping-off point for more speculation in the days to come.

After another hour of pacing, Rosalinda stepped into the barn, lit a coal-oil lantern, and set it on the table. For a split second she saw Hector's face sharpening the talon blades for his fighting cocks. Then Dr. Pierce's words echoed in her head, "Hector has a better chance of getting into heaven."

Walking over to Zuzu, she placed her head against his. He seemed to sense the ache in her heart, let out a sigh, and then gently leaned his head into hers.

She wrapped both arms around his neck and said, "You and Shakespeare are the only ones who could love me without fear of retribution." This time when she started to cry she did not fight back the tears. She cried holding onto her friend until she only had enough energy to whimper, then there was nothing left but a dull ache.

Rosalinda patted Zuzu then stepped back. He gave a gentle neigh and nodded his head when she picked a towel off a hook and wiped off the wet spots left by her tears.

She put out the lantern and making her way back to the house, she stopped for a moment to look up at the moon. It was a full moon casting a light blue hue on the ground. The overflowing dam of anguish had burst, and she was grateful for it; maybe now she could think clearly. She wished Shakespeare was here, so he could comfort her with his heartbeat and warm body.

She did not expect to sleep when she collapsed onto the bed she had shared with her sister but fell asleep almost immediately.

When she awoke, she realized by the height of the sun it had to be close to noon. Part of her wanted to stay in bed and pretend everything was the same as a few days ago.

As she lay on her pillow, she heard a bird singing from the tree by the barn. Then she softly said, "What would my mother and father think of me? Would they still love me? Would Cecelia?" A moment later the bird flew away and she heard the flap of its wings as it passed over the house.

It was like a signal that she should get up, wash up, and force down some nourishment. She knew she needed a plan and couldn't afford the luxury of wallowing in pain.

After eating some canned peaches, she pulled out a few pieces of paper from her satchel and started outlining her plan.

Rosalinda calmly opened the door to Silas' office at one-thirty. He was reading the newspaper with one foot propped up on the open lower desk drawer.

He stood and then straightened up looking slightly embarrassed. Rosalinda pretended she didn't notice.

"Anything worth reading today?" Rosalinda casually asked.

"No, not much. They did mention yesterday's automobile accident and Bower's death." Silas smiled and added, "Oh well, I guess that's just how it goes sometimes."

Rosalinda quickly concocted a reply, "Those machines do look dangerous. It would be a nice improvement if they could build one with horse sense; a horse knows when it's too close to the side of the road."

"Amen to that." Silas cheerfully responded. "So, what can I do for you?"

"Well, I'm sure you know that Mr. Bowers had been taking care of my mother's estate."

"Yes, I know. I guess this kinda complicates things."

"Yes, it does, at least in the short term. Another lawyer is taking over very soon, so I am not overly concerned."

Silas nodded in agreement as she continued.

"However, the reason I am here is that Mr. Bowers' brother in San Francisco was in the process of finding my sister Cecelia. I understand from Dr. Pierce that you had wired him. But, I'm afraid that I don't know how to contact him."

"Oh sure, I can give you that information. I got it from Dan Edwards over at Bowers' office yesterday. You know, to officially notify the next of kin."

As he scratched down the information on a three by five card, Rosalinda casually added, "It's a shame. He sure did a lot for me. I told Dr. Pierce that I wouldn't be at ease if he didn't have a regular resting place. I hope his brother takes his remains, if not, I could do something for him I suppose." She paused to read his face – he almost looked convinced.

"Anyway, my mother was very superstitious. She believed that if someone dies and they never knew that you were thankful for whatever they did for you, even if they were bad people, well they would either come back to haunt you or you would have very bad luck. Well, I never thanked him – not properly." She paused for another second, "Do you think I'm crazy? My mother was always right about everything else."

Silas pulled at his ear, "My father had some funny ideas too, you know, the older I get, the more I believe he was right on just about everything." He handed her the piece of paper and added, "If you do end up burying him, you might want to get him over to Santa Rosa. Some people 'round here might find it entertaining to vandalize his gravesite."

"You are right, thank you, I hadn't thought of that."

"Could you tell me if his brother," she looked down at the piece of paper, "what's his name, Calvin, will be contacting you or someone else when he's made a decision about the remains?"

"Oh, that would be Dr. Pierce. Maybe he's already heard something."

"Well you've been a big help. Give my best to your family."

"Glad I could help. You have a good day now."

As she shut the door she thought, "I already concluded that his gravesite could be vandalized. Now Silas thinks it was his idea and that's good, very good."

When she reached Dr. Pierce's place he was just climbing into his buggy. "Hello Rosalinda. Sorry I can't visit with you, I'm on my way to check on Ned Weaver again."

"Just a quick question; did you hear from Mr. Bowers' brother?"

"Well, yes I did. He would like the body shipped to San Francisco."

"I see. That's very good." Rosalinda replied.

"Except it's on the condition that the body is escorted on the train."

Rosalinda looked puzzled, "What does an escort do?"

"Oh, they don't have to sit with the body. They just need to be on the train so that if anything unusual happens, the railroad company has an immediate contact. He is willing to give the escort first class accommodations. I'd take it myself, but I'm pretty tied up around here."

Rosalinda rubbed her chin then snapped her fingers as if a great idea magically popped into her head, "You know Cecelia is somewhere out there in San Francisco, maybe I could be the escort. If I was there, I'd have better luck finding her."

"I suppose so. Well if you decide to do it, let the undertaker know. He can get everything set up for proper transportation. You know I think it would be a good thing for you to experience a big city at least once; it'll open your eyes to a different world. Not necessarily better, but certainly different."

Rosalinda nodded as if to contemplate what he was saying then replied, "You may be right. Well, I don't want to keep you any longer. Maybe we should make an appointment for some lemonade – we've sure been missing each other lately."

"Appointment? Bah, I got away from the city to avoid that sort of thing." He gave the horse a gentle slap of the reins, waved goodbye, and was soon well down the street.

Rosalinda turned then walked the two short blocks east and one block south of the main street to Sutton's Mortuary.

Like many of the town's businesses, Sutton's Mortuary was connected to part of his house, it sat on a corner lot slightly larger than most. As she got closer she noticed that there was an entry for the discrete delivery of remains at the back of the building. She stepped onto the front porch where she found a sign on the front door, "Come in. If you don't see me, come around back and ring the bell."

She entered and called out, "Hello? Are you here Mr. Sutton, Stan?" No answer.

The Sutton family had been in the undertaking business in Oklahoma for generations. Stan had two older brothers who were ready to take over the business. He either had to go into another line of work or venture out on his own to make a decent living.

Stan, now in his early thirties, was friendly, and oddly, had the athletic physique of a strong ranch hand. Perhaps that's why people took a liking to him despite his vocation.

She peeked inside the large parlor used for viewing; it was empty save for three rows of chairs facing a blank wall. Rosalinda closed the front door behind her and made her way to

the back where a structure, about the size of a medium barn, had been added to the house.

She remembered Mr. Sutton saying that "wild west" attitudes were great for his business though it made him feel a bit guilty. Perhaps that is why whenever someone died due to foul play, Stan sent a portion of his fees to Dr. Pierce to use for emergency medical supplies for the poor. Rosalinda wondered if part of Mr. Sutton's fees for Mr. Bowers would be considered "wild west."

At the door she pulled on a chain ringing a bell inside the building. Mr. Sutton answered the door a few moments later. "Ah, come in Rosalinda," he said while taking off his oil-cloth apron. "What can I do for you? Can I get you some coffee? I made a fresh pot."

She stepped inside a simple, nicely decorated room displaying several coffins ranging from simple pine to high-end glossy cherry wood. A door to the right lead to the main house and another door behind the coffins, opened into his working area; where Ben was now.

In the corner sat a roll top desk, a matching chair, and nearby, two wooden chairs against the wall. In another corner a small potbellied stove and fresh pot of coffee made the room feel cozy despite the coffins.

Rosalinda forced a smile and said, "The coffee smells great but I'm afraid I only have time for half a cup and I've been fighting a headache for most of the morning."

"I thought you looked a little down. Maybe the coffee will help." Stan noticed that there was only one cup on the shelf. "Oh shoot. I'll be right back with another cup."

"Oh, you don't have to do that for a half cup."

"Don't be silly. I could use a little company," he said as he disappeared into the house.

Rosalinda moved closer to the stove warming her hands. Although it was nearly two o'clock in the afternoon, the air was unusually cool, and she hadn't thought to bring a wrap. She turned her head and saw a picture on the wall. With a closer look she saw it was a photograph of the Sutton Family Funeral Home with the family posed on the front steps. For some reason it recalled a conversation with Cecelia as they hung out the wash. "That Mr. Sutton is sweet on you Rosalinda," she teased. "He's handsome and wouldn't be a bad catch if you don't mind living with ghosts."

Stan came back with the cup and a plate of shortbread cookies. "Here's a cup, and in case you're a little hungry, I brought some cookies." He put down the plate and poured her exactly half a cup. "Is black okay?"

"Yes, black is fine." She took the cup and sat down.

Stan poured himself a cup, moved his chair to face her and sat down.

He leaned slightly forward, smiled broadly, and said, "Well then, what can I do for you?"

Rosalinda took a sip and held the warm cup between her hands. "The coffee is very good, thank you." Then she took another sip and placed the cup down on the desk. "I just learned from Dr. Pierce that Ben Bower's brother wants his brother to be buried in San Francisco. However, it is on the condition that the remains have an escort on the train."

Stan straightened up with obvious curiosity. "Yes, that's true enough, under the circumstances of his demise, it's not likely anyone would volunteer for the job."

"I would. I mean I am."

"What, why?"

Rosalinda steadied herself. "I think I will have a cookie," she said as she took one off the plate. "It's a bit of a long story. As you and likely the whole town probably know, Cecelia left home a while back to get away from my stepfather."

"Yes, I heard she left, but didn't know the particulars."

Rosalinda took a bite of the cookie, a sip of coffee, and then continued, "It took some time, but I finally learned that she was going to San Francisco."

Stan nodded that he was following along.

"Mr. Bowers, who was my attorney, volunteered to contact his brother Calvin, who is also an attorney, to see if he could track her down for me." She took another sip of coffee and another bite of cookie.

Stan took a sip as well then said, "so, if you accompany the body, Calvin Bowers is more likely to put further energy into the search. And, if you're physically there, he is less likely to put you on the back burner."

"Exactly right!" Rosalinda exclaimed. For good measure she added, "Besides, I understand Calvin is picking up all the travel expenses."

"Yes, first-class accommodations." Stan turned to his desk and picked up the telegram. "It says that the escort would receive a round-trip first-class rail ticket, two weeks lodgings in San Francisco, and two-hundred dollars." He put the paper down. "I would have done this myself, but I'm already committed to two funerals this week on top of getting Mr. Bowers packed."

There was something unnerving about the humor in Stan's voice when he said, "getting Mr. Bowers packed." Rosalinda needed some assurance.

"Now Stan, it's real important to me that the body look its best for his family. You know what I mean. If his brother's remains are in poor shape he may not be inclined to help me find my sister." She put her hand lightly on top of his, then moved it away as if she had accidently touched him.

"I understand Rosalinda. You can be sure I'll have him looking as good as any mortuary in San Francisco. In fact, I'll go over to his room and pick out his best suit."

"Thank you. When will he be ready? I have no idea how long these things take."

234

"Actually, I have most of the challenging work done. I checked the train schedule on the outside chance there would be an escort and I can have him ready for the one o'clock train tomorrow afternoon. I could move it out another day if you need more time, but he may not look as good."

"No, tomorrow is just fine." Rosalinda replied.

"All right then, I'll meet you at the station at twelve-thirty to give you the proper paperwork. I'll also send a message this afternoon to let Calvin Bowers know you are the escort."

By four o'clock she was sitting at her mother's kitchen table reviewing her list for the third time, "Did I leave anything out? Will it work? Will anyone suspect that I'm leaving for Hattie's sake?"

She nervously tapped the end of her pencil while mentally reviewing her actions:

Convince enough people that there are credible reasons to leave town. Done.

Dr. Pierce: He's all for me seeing a big city while looking for my sister. Silas: He thinks I should take heed of my mother's superstitions. Stan: Keep in good stead with Ben's brother so he might help me search for Cecelia. Mr. Hatcher: Same reason given Stan; and gave him Calvin's address for forwarding mail.

Get funds from bank for travel and two month's living expenses. Buy a suitcase. Done.

Withdrawal made. The bank manager said, if needed, the Bank of America in San Francisco could wire him a request for additional funds. He also understands need to work with Ben's brother in person.

Care of animals and gardens: Done.

Told Lourdes' family they can have the chickens and the goat. There's enough feed to last them for several months. Told Mateo that he could have the vegetables already growing at my mother's place. He needs to continue to care for the Curtis place. Explained to Mr. Hatcher how the proceeds are to be split between the boy and Earl for produce from the Curtis place. Mateo gets all proceeds from my mother's garden. Also, told them the same story I told Silas.

Figure out what to tell Hattie: Not Done!

What can I tell Hattie? How do I, can I, say goodbye? I need to tell her what happened to Ben, how do I tell her all the details? What do I say about Father Palo?

Nineteen – A Pair of Hankies

Hattie, who just finished cultivating the last row of squash, stood admiring her work. All the plants had grown substantially since Rosalinda's arrival, and now their rich green leaves were bursting with promise. Even the green beans started to find their way up the carefully strung trellises as if to say, "I'm ready to live – my reach is limitless!" Standing there, she felt as if Rosalinda was present and smiling at her. She regained all her strength and weight and her energy was at a level she had not felt in what seemed years. She looked out over the garden and whispered, "I feel just like you."

She had propped her hoe against the side of the house when Lourdes came out of the house. "Señora Curtis, the babies drank all their goat milk and now they are sleeping. Do you want me to do anything more before I go?"

Hattie gently placed her hand on top of the girl's head, "no, but thank you for asking. You can go now."

Hattie watched as Lourdes headed towards home. Walking to the barn, she checked to make sure the burro and laying hens had plenty of feed and water. Shakespeare suddenly bounded from around the back of the barn and began to playfully romp about her. He kicked up dust and barked softly until she stopped to give

him some attention. "Oh, you're such silly puppy. All right, but only for a minute." She sat on a wooden crate and held his handsome head between her hands, scratching behind his ears.

"I know you miss her." He lowered his rump to sit while Hattie continued to pet him. "I miss her too; more than I can tell anyone except you and that milk goat over there. I wonder what's taking her so long. At any rate, it can't be good news for Ben if she needed to be gone last night and all day today. Do you think she'll be home for supper?" She gave him a couple of pats on the head and then checked on the chickens and gave the goat a section of alfalfa and the pile of weeds she'd pulled out of the garden earlier.

When she was done she noticed that Shakespeare was waiting right where she left him. "Come on boy, I may as well feed you now."

The last of twilight was nearly gone when Hattie heard Zuzu's slow canter towards the barn. Looking out the window, she watched Rosalinda effortlessly dismount the great horse and then headed out to meet her.

"Can I help?" Hattie cheerfully asked, looking at the full cloth sacks hanging from the saddle.

Rosalinda pulled off the two sacks on one side of the horse, "Here, go ahead and take these. I'll be in as soon as I take care of Zuzu."

Hattie tried to read Rosalinda's face, but it was too dark. She took the bundles from Rosalinda. "All right," she said then quickly added, "Don't take too long."

Hattie put water on the stove for tea and was reaching for the cups when Rosalinda stepped in. "I can make you something to eat if you're..." Hattie stopped mid-sentence when she saw a new suitcase in Rosalinda's hand.

"What is it? What's going on?" She searched Rosalinda's face for answers and felt her heart sink.

Rosalinda stayed calm even though her emotional core could unravel at any moment. "Were you going to make us tea? I could use a nice cup." As she placed the suitcase on the floor, Hattie could barely tear her eyes away from it. "Hattie, maybe a couple of those dried apricots would be good."

A few seconds passed as Rosalinda took a seat at the table. Hattie heard the water start to boil and forced herself to prepare the tea. She placed the mason jar of dried apricots on the table.

"Please, sit down Hattie." Rosalinda gently touched Hattie's hand. "Quite a bit has happened."

Rosalinda spoke slowly as she cautiously recounted most, but not all, of the events of the past two days: Ben's condition, how and why it happened, and Father Palo's departure without mentioning her role in it. As she spoke she carefully watched Hattie's reactions; would she take sides with the town's people, would she be repulsed by Ben's attraction to another man, or would she feel that Ben and Father Palo betrayed her trust by pretending to be "normal" around her?

"That's awful, that's just awful!" Hattie exclaimed, "It's disgusting."

Rosalinda swallowed hard and felt the walls of her heart collapsing. She bowed her head, concealing any facial expression.

"Ben Bowers was a good man." Hattie cried out.

Rosalinda snapped her head up in amazement.

"How could they do that to him?" Hattie continued, "I wouldn't care if he wore ribbons in his hair, had his own doll house, or washed Father Palo's back on Saturday night!" She plopped down on the chair holding a dishcloth against her face as she cried.

Rosalinda placed her right arm around Hattie's shoulders, tilted her head upon hers and gently rocked. Then, Hattie took Rosalinda's other hand in hers and softly stroked it as if it were as fragile as a day-old chick.

Now that it was safe to talk about Ben and Father Palo with a little more openness, Rosalinda added, "I got Father Palo safely on the train to St. Louis and gave him enough money to get by until he finds another line of work. If you ever receive a communication from a Sam Lewis, that's him."

Hattie's tears had stopped, and she wiped her nose and eyes with one hand while keeping Rosalinda's hand enclosed with the other.

Hattie cleared her throat and asked, "So, what's going to happen to Ben's remains?"

"Everyone around here would be very happy to just dump him in the ravine where they found him. Silas said that any grave would be vandalized by kids or drunks. But…," Rosalinda took a breath, "fortunately Ben's brother is paying to have his remains taken all the way to San Francisco. The only hitch was that the body had to be escorted."

"Who would do that?" A moment of silence passed, "You would, wouldn't you? That's the reason for the new suitcase."

"Yes."

"How long will you be gone?"

Rosalinda stood up and poured more hot water in her cup. She hated to pull herself away from Hattie's touch, but knew it was necessary. The truthful answer "forever" felt like a dam full of tears about to overflow; but she had to keep it all in. She stared at her cup for courage.

"I don't know what the situation will be when I get there. I have the last address for Cecelia, so finding her should be no problem. She may want to return, or maybe she wants to see other parts of the country for a while. Since I'm there, maybe I can spend time being a tourist."

Rosalinda took a swallow to help her take control of her faltering voice, "I made arrangements for Zuzu's care, but wasn't sure if you would want to take care of Shakespeare." With tremendous effort, she got the words out without them breaking apart. She knew she would have to leave her beloved friend behind – perhaps forever.

"Of course, I'll take care of him."

Rosalinda was relieved to hear this and was also relieved to hear the babies began to stir in the other room and see Hattie get up to care for them.

For the rest of the evening they talked about caring for the ranch – what needed to be done in the garden, care of the animals, Lourdes, Mateo, and the stock of food in the root cellar. Rosalinda wanted to share her deep, heartfelt words tonight, but knew there would never be a right time or place to do so. It was better this way; it was the only way.

Rosalinda barely dozed and was awakened to the hoot of a barn owl well before dawn. For a few moments she just stared at the ceiling, hoping it all was a terrible dream; but it was not. She got up, put on her old serape, and walked out into the brisk morning air.

Hearing her come through the door, Shakespeare awoke and came out of his house to greet her.

When she saw him her heart immediately broke. Oh, how she loved him. Wiping her eyes, she placed her serape in his house, and then reached to scratch him behind the ears. For some unexplained reason, he whimpered.

For a moment she thought he was injured, but quickly determined he was not. He looked back at the serape and whimpered again. It was too much to bear. How did he know?

She sat on the ground next to him, held him tight, and in low, pain-filled moans she cried, "I'm sorry, I'm so sorry. I'm sorry, I'm so sorry. I have to leave; it's the only way for all of us."

When her tears were finally spent, Rosalinda got up from the ground and washed her face at the pump. The sun would be up soon, and she wanted to be packed before Hattie was up and about. She figured it would be less painful if she departed right after breakfast rather than feeling Hattie watching her as she packed.

It didn't take long to gather what she wanted. Now, save for closing the lid and securing the leather buckles, she was done. Except for what she would wear, she packed all her new clothing. She had already thrown out her old clothes so the only things indicating she was ever here was the cot and underneath it, a pair of work shoes, heavy leather gloves, and a straw hat.

Since she would ride Zuzu back to town, she dressed in a pair of new trousers and shirt. And then, as if it was a normal morning, Rosalinda prepared a pot of coffee and had the biscuits ready.

By seven o'clock Rosalinda heard Hattie finishing up with the children and handed her a cup when she came out of the bedroom.

"How are the children this morning?" Rosalinda asked.

"They're just fine. I swear they were a lot smaller when they went to sleep last night. I'm sure they will look quite different when you see them again."

"Yes, I'm sure they will grow quite a bit." Rosalinda said as she poured herself a cup then brought the biscuits and jam to the table."

They both sat down and half-heartedly ate, saying very little.

"Did you pack anything to eat? I can get some things together for you."

"Yes, I've got some biscuits, a jar of peaches, and I'm afraid I took one of your spoons."

She was about to close the suitcase when Hattie handed her a beautifully embroidered hankie.

"My mother gave me a pair of these. I'd like to think that when you are lonely you can take this out and think fondly of us, where ever you are."

Rosalinda, taking the hankie, softly stroked the fine embroidery, "Thank you, I will. I always will." She gently placed it in the suitcase and secured the buckles.

Shakespeare was waiting outside. Rosalinda only gave him a quick scratch and said, "You have the watch boy, just be careful not to bite Earl by mistake."

Once she finished hanging her luggage and a sack of food from the saddle, she stepped towards Hattie.

Hattie said, "You be careful in that big city and write to me when you can."

"I'll write you when I get there. Don't let yourself get run down again. Promise me."

"I promise."

They both leaned in, giving each other a long embrace. "Well I best be off," Rosalinda said, fighting to hide the tell-tale tears as she released herself from Hattie's arms and climbed into the saddle.

"I'll miss you." Hattie said in earnest as if she was trying to get Rosalinda's attention. Rosalinda looked down and saw the sincerity on Hattie's face as she said once again, softer, "I will miss you Rosalinda."

Rosalinda's eyes welled up again and this time started to overflow. Her heart was breaking, and she could barely generate her words to reply, "I'll miss you too." Then she quickly turned Zuzu's head towards town and sped away.

That evening Hattie sat outside and gently scratched behind Shakespeare's ears. As the rising moon emerged into view she pondered, "It just finished coming up in Amarillo. I wonder if Rosalinda can see it yet?" Then she looked down at her friend and asked, "Shall we stay a little longer? Maybe Rosalinda will look out from her train window, gaze up at the moon and know we're thinking of her at the same time. I bet she could feel it; don't you?" He stood up to reposition himself and laid down with his upper body leaning against her leg.

As the trained banked north, Rosalinda forced herself to look east for the first time since leaving. She was fearful that should she look back she would not be able to control her tears or govern the pent-up sobs. Now that she could barely discern the landscape she focused on the bright full moon and remembered the coyotes crying out as they searched for one another.

It was not her original intention to sit in the very back of the car, but now she was grateful for it. After several stops, only a few passengers remained towards the front and they would not feel obligated to talk to her.

She let the tears silently run down her cheeks and then furtively daubed them with Hattie's hankie. She told herself to focus on finding Cecelia, but the tears did not stop. She told herself to think about what happened to Ben; surely Hattie will be better without her near. At some point she would break, the secrets of her heart would be clear, and Hattie could be appalled. Then what? Yes, it's better that she left before the damage was done.

Rosalinda took out another handkerchief, blew her nose and looked back at the moon. What if, by some implausible miracle, Hattie loved me too? Could there be a way? Would there be a way?

To Be Continued…

In the early 1900's the New Mexico Territory was still the wild west. If the town of Tucumcari learned of the attraction between Rosalinda and Hattie, would they become outcasts or even face death? Can they possibly reveal their deep love for each other? Will they find a way to be together?

Hattie and Rosalinda continue their brave journeys through turbulent times in *Hattie's Homestead - Book Two.*